A PULP FICTION MAGAZINE | ISSUE #3

LITERARY OUTLAW

IN THIS ISSUE:

LITERARY OUTLAW #3
Copyright © 2024 by LiteraryOutlawLLC

Front Cover - Vintage Kellogg's Phoney Face (modified) | Public Domain
The Man Who Did Nothing | Copyright © 2004, 2023 by Karen Traviss. Used by permission.
Previously published in *Realms of Fantasy, June 2003, Year's Best Fantasy & Horror #17.*
Honourable Mention, Year's Best Science Fiction #21
Page 17 - Painting by Matt Fox, from *Weird Tales, March 1949* | Public Domain
Richard Cory | Public Domain
Starchild | Public Domain. Originally published in *Nightmare #14*
The Summer of Grunge | Copyright © 2014, 2024 by LiteraryOutlawLLC
Previously published as *No. 38*
The Tormented One | Public Domain. Art by Elder. Originally published in *Psycho #7*
The Bridge of San Luis Rey | Public Domain. Originally published in 1927
Firehair | Public Domain. Originally published in *Ranger Comics #21*
Penrod | Public Domain. Originally published in 1914
Gratitude On A Very Dark Night | Public Domain. Originally published in *Tense Suspense #2*
The Anvil of Jove | Copyright © 1978 by Steven Riddle. Originally published in *Phoebe Issue 8.1, 1978*

www.literaryoutlaw.com

THE MAN WHO DID NOTHING

BY KAREN TRAVISS

HURSLEY RISE, MAY 2

There was a boy - five, maybe six - sitting on half a discarded mattress by the kerb as Jeff drove down the road. At first he thought the child was trying to open a bottle of pop, but the closer he got, the better he could see that the boy was making a petrol bomb.

Jeff slowed to a crawl and then stopped. He didn't dare switch the engine off, not here. A daffodil nodded in the grass at the side of the road and the whine of a power-drill competed intermittently with music throbbing from an open window. The normality didn't reassure him; he opened the car window about six inches.

The child was trying to thread some rags into the neck of a beer bottle, pausing every so often to hold the bottle up to the light, sigh, and resume his task of working the rag into the neck of the bottle with his index finger.

For a moment Jeff thought about getting out and taking the thing from him. Then an older boy in the latest Manchester United tracksuit walked up to the kid and crouched over him, like a protective elder brother, and took the bottle gently from him. He examined the wick, pushed it further into the bottle and handed it back to the kid.

That was how you did it. Then both boys looked up at Jeff, as if moving as one.

"Antichrist! Fuckin' Antichrist!" they shouted. And the bottle - unlit, mercifully - arced and crashed onto the road just short of the driver's door. Both boys ran back up the road, not looking back.

He could have - *should have* - got out of the car and taken the lethal little toy from the kid. He should have marched him back to his own front door and berated his mother for letting such a tiny child handle potential destruction. He should have done something.

But he didn't. It was Hursley Rise, and these were dangerous times, and the shabby little housing estate was going mad. He accelerated away towards the city center.

HURSLEY RISE CITIZENS' DROP-IN CENTER, NINE DAYS EARLIER.

"I don't see why he should be living next door to me," said the woman in the interview booth. She smelled of chip fat and Issey Miyake perfume: in the small plaster-boarded space the combination was distracting.

"""

"He's the Antichrist. Can't you do something about it? Get him moved or something?"

It wasn't an unusual request to make of your ward councilor. Since Jeff Blake had started holding evening surgeries at the community center, he had seen two constituents complaining about military radar upsetting their racing pigeons, and a man who had lined his loft with cooking foil to stop military intelligence beaming messages into his home. He had wanted an improvement grant to pay for lead sheet, just to be on the safe side.

"How do you know he's the Antichrist, Mrs. Avery?" Jeff asked. He caught the inside of his cheek discreetly between his teeth to stifle a laugh. You couldn't mock a voter a week before an election. "I mean, we can't just go in and evict the bloke like that. The courts will want some grounds for action."

"He's evil. Pure evil."

"Well, lots of people aren't very loveable, Mrs. Avery. It doesn't make them the devil."

"Since he moved in there's been nothing but trouble in our road. He's a weird old sod. Lives on his own. The kids are terrified of him."

"Yes, but why do you think he's the Antichrist?" She looked at him for a brief blank moment, as if the word had thrown her. Then she puffed a sigh and began rummaging in her bag. While her head was tilted down, he could see the darker roots in her red spiky hair. A packet of low-tar cigarettes and the latest, tiniest, slimmest mobile phone clattered onto the melamine table while she excavated.

"There," she said at last. And she handed him a creased strip of newspaper.

The headline was from one of the tabloids: ANTICHRIST WILL APPEAR ON COUNCIL ESTATE, WARNS RECLUSE. The story reported the ramblings of a man who predicted the new millennium would see the arrival of the Beast in a humble home. The man, said the story, had no electricity, phone or mains water but kept track of world events by communing with the cosmic consciousness on his allotment. He claimed the Antichrist would be identified by the trail of havoc he left behind him.

Jeff handed the cutting back to Mrs. Avery. "I thought it was 666," he said.

"What is?"

"The identifying mark of Satan."

Mrs. Avery scowled. She had one of those flat, hard little faces with thin lips and broad noses, the prevailing type on the estate. Inbred, he decided. Whining and helpless: it wasn't a view he would voice, not even to his wife Bev. He wished secretly for the working class of his dad's generation, skilled manual workers with scrubbed front doorsteps, all neat proud poverty and a horror of hire purchase.

"You'll laugh the other side of your bleedin' face when he starts," she said. She stood and slung her bag over her shoulder. "And don't expect me to vote for you, neither. I'm coming back with a petition."

Hers was just one vote. He had a seven thousand majority here, even if the party was holding on to overall control of the council by just one seat. And, as leader, he was assured a safe one. He watched her departing back with no regrets. "Silly cow," he said to himself.

He gathered up his papers to go home. He was on time. He wouldn't have to grab a takeaway as a peace offering to a huffy Bev, silently angry after yet another dinner left to congeal in the oven on a low heat.

While he was fumbling in his briefcase for his car keys, his phone warbled. He put the case on the roof of the car and took the phone – clunkier, older, less desirable than mad Mrs. Avery's chic device – from his jacket.

"Jeff Blake."

"Jeff, it's Warren. We've got a bit of a problem."

"Christ, when haven't we?" He could hear bar sounds in the background. "Are you in the staff club?"

"Yeah."

"I thought you were supposed to be out canvassing for Graham. Some poxy deputy you are - "

"Well, this is about Graham." Rustling noises and a sudden drop in the background noise suggested Warren had moved somewhere secluded. "He's in a spot of trouble."

"What now? Drink driving?"

"Computer porn. Accessed using the council network."

"Who knows about it?"

"Only a few people. IT staff, internal audit and the chief executive."

"Okay, first thing in the morning, I want you and him in my office. First thing, mind. I want it sorted."

Jeff got in the car and sat for a few minutes in despairing silence before turning the key and moving off. A slithering noise above his head followed by a dull thud made him hit the brakes. He looked in the rear view mirror: his briefcase, split open by the fall from the car roof, was scattering papers to the breeze.

"Oh, bollocks," he said. And Mrs. Avery's Antichrist seemed like an easier problem to deal with right then.

MEMO

To: Head of Housing Service
From: Hursley Area Housing Manager
Re: 15 Barton Crescent

We have had six more complaints from tenants today asking us to evict Michael Warburton of 15 Barton Crescent on the basis that he is the Antichrist. We have also had a similar complaint from an owner-occupier in Waverley Gardens about Frank James Morton of Flat 35. My staff have explained we have no power to evict if there is no breach of the tenancy agreement, and that they can't both be the Antichrist. I know these people have unusual views but we are aware there is talk of "doing the job" themselves. I would appreciate some support and advice on the situation before it boils over.

There was a Victorian oil painting of a former lord mayor hanging in the corridor leading to Jeff's office at the town hall. It always bothered him. As he walked closer, he could see a grotesque, round-faced figure with cartoon-like circular eyes, and as he drew level with it the face resolved into grim patriarchal realism. He knew it was just the light playing on the swirls and textures of the oil paint. But these days all things seemed sinister, imbued with darker meaning.

Graham Vance was already sitting in the office, looking for all the world like a schoolboy in need of a good slap. His face looked like the years had been put on it by a make-up artist, creped and puffed and grayed on top of youth, as if he could be restored to his boyish prettiness by just peeling it all off.

Go on, cower, you little shit, Jeff thought. *I'll teach you to risk this party's majority.* He leaned forward and braced his elbows on his desk.

"Why the hell did you do this through the council network? You know it's monitored."

Graham shrugged. "So what have I done?"

"Downloading child porn."

"No way."

"You've e-mailed pictures to all your noncey mates, too. Don't lie to me."

Vance looked slightly thrown. He pulled a dismissive face. "It's a private matter. And it was just pictures, only teenagers. It's not as if I've been caught with a little kid, is it?"

"I don't believe what I'm hearing. You make me sick."

"Prove I've done something illegal."

"Someone probably could, but what worries me most is what it looks like to the voters." Jeff glanced down the print-out on his desk: line after line, thousands of them, of www's and .coms and incomprehensible things - except for words like *ripe schoolgirls* and *Toilet Boy*. "You're on one of the social services sub-committees. What are you going to do?"

"Do I have to do anything?"

"I'd suggest you resign but it's too close to the election and we'd have to explain you away to the media."

Graham didn't appear contrite. "Fuss about bugger all, really."

"Really? Like the drink-driving, and the prostitute on the civic trip to France?"

"It's pretty harmless stuff. Nothing extreme."

"I wouldn't know, and I'm not much inclined to look at it, either. That's Audit's job. You're a disaster waiting to happen for this party." Jeff gave up trying to stare him into an apology and leaned back in his chair. "After the election, if we get back in - if you get back in - "

"You need my seat to keep overall control of this council," Graham said. "You want the opposition to walk in? This is dirty washing we can do in private." He paused. "You can talk the chief exec out of taking this to the Standards Committee, can't you?"

"Can't promise," Jeff said, hearing himself bluff and hating himself for it. "Now piss off and don't let me hear another word out of you."

He sat alone in his office with the door shut for a long time after Graham had left, and tried to clear his correspondence. So men looked at porn on the net: it was human nature. With any luck, Graham might not have done anything criminal. He'd see the chief internal auditor later, just to make sure he knew the size of the problem.

But it was time he should have been out canvassing. One-seat majorities didn't look after themselves.

PETITION

From the Residents Action Committee of Hursley Rise
To Dennington Vale Borough Council

We the undersigned want the Antichrist and his accomplices off of our estate so decent people can live in peace and safety. We know who they are and where they are. We have a list of them. They should not be living near families. If the council don't get them out then we will.

The phone rang.

"Answer the bloody thing," Bev growled into her pillow, and pulled the duvet up over her head. Jeff looked at the alarm clock: it wasn't quite midnight. The voice on the end of the phone was a reporter from the local paper.

"Have you got any comment on the riots, Councilor Blake?"

At first the words didn't register. Jeff turned the word *riot* round in his mind. "What riot?"

"I thought you'd know about it by now. They're setting fire to houses at Hursley Rise and there's a running battle between police and residents. About a hundred and twenty coppers there now."

Jeff found himself drowning in panic. *Porn scandal, breakdown of law and order, media circus, election disaster.* "I'll get back to you," he said, and slammed the phone down.

He was into his clothes and halfway down the path to the garage when he remembered he had left without telling Bev where he was going, or even knowing which road he was heading for.

But as he drove closer to Hursley he couldn't miss the glow of a blaze outlining the youth activities center, or the police vans heading away from it with their blue lights strobing. The last one to pass him bore the livery of the neighboring county's force: they must have called for reinforcements. A klaxon behind him made him pull over, and a fire engine sped past him, clipping the bollard in the center of the road.

Even two streets away, he could hear dogs barking, glass smashing, occasional cheers. It sounded like a football match. And then he could smell it - petrol, smoke, and diesel exhaust. He rounded the corner by the eight-till-late, where two men were hammering boards across a shattered window, and slowed to a creep.

A dull thud on the back window made him brake hard. The car stalled.

He swung round in his seat, expecting a mob and missiles, but there was nothing. Then someone rapped hard on the passenger side window.

"Jesus -"

"Jeff, turn round. Are you bloody insane?" It was Gwen Hillier, another of the three Hursley Rise ward councilors. He wound down the window. She was pointing frantically, like a crazed race marshal. "I said turn round. Park down Stanley Street."

It took Gwen a few minutes to catch up with him. She leaned on her stick and struggled for breath. The dim red glow shone off the rims of her spectacles.

"I've lived here sixty years and I've never seen them go off like this," she said. "Not that you'd know that, living in Vale End. I've had to run for it. Me! They went berserk and started pointing and saying it was the council's fault for moving them in."

"Who's them? The hordes of Satan?"

"Don't joke. Get round to Barton Crescent and take a look. They won't recognize you, will they?"

I am the Leader of the Council, Jeff thought. *They'll expect me to do something statesmanlike.* He set off at a jog towards the center of the estate, slowing sooner than he expected to a wheezing half-walk, half-stumble: middle-age wasn't treating him as well as he had imagined. And then, when he reached the junction of Barton Crescent and the main road through the estate, he saw a scene straight from Hieronymus Bosch.

A small van was lying on its side, ablaze. A fire crew was playing a hose on it, retreating every few seconds under a hail of bricks and bottles from a group of youths. Behind them, another crew was trying to get into a house where flames were spitting from a ground-floor window. A cordon of police with visors and riot shields were forcing back screaming residents to clear a path. Everywhere Jeff looked, there were ugly little cameos of violence and destruction, and a disturbing number of small children picking up debris where it fell and hurling it back into the melee.

And there were TV cameras. Jeff spotted them just after they spotted him. A cameraman and a reporter sprinted across to him, dodging bottles.

"Councilor Blake, what do you make of this?"

Jeff couldn't see past the brilliant white light perched on top of the camera, and all he could think of was how scruffy he must have looked without a collar and tie.

"It's - it's an outrage," he said. The autopilot that drove all politicians took over. "This is the work of a few hotheads, probably not even locals."

"But what do you say to people who claim you've allowed the Antichrist to move on to an estate full of families and have ignored pleas to move him out?"

"I say it's complete garbage in this day and age. This isn't the Middle Ages. It's just an excuse for drunken vandalism and I can promise a full enquiry."

The light snapped off, leaving him blinking at yellow after-images, and he was alone again in a sea of chaos.

A roar went up and a group of police moved in a wave towards the Waverley Gardens tower block in pursuit of a mob, who appeared to have another target in mind.

He paused for a second and felt helpless. An inner voice said *do something*, but nothing practical came to mind. A brick shattered into fragments a few feet from him and he snapped out of the stupor and made a dash for the car.

He'd never seen anything like it. There would be hell to pay in the morning.

The police superintendent walked towards him, flanked by two sergeants. She wiped her brow on the back of one hand, checker-braided cap in the other. "Glad I caught you," she said. "The place has gone mad. Where's all this Antichrist stuff come from?"

"Bloody media," Jeff said. "Bloody media."

★ ★ ★

NEWS HEADLINES
WEDNESDAY, APRIL 25

Fifty arrested in Hursley Rise "Antichrist" riots

Twenty police treated in hospital

Two homes looted and burned after residents flee

Tenants action group threatens to picket town hall to get "devil men" evicted.

★ ★ ★

There was a Japanese film crew waiting on the steps up to the town hall's grand Palladian portico. Jeff watched them for a few minutes from the window of the conference room.

"Look at them all," said the chief executive. "They've set up satellite links at the back of the building too."

"Can't complain we're not on the map now, can we, Lennie?" Jeff sat down and leafed through a pile of morning papers, most bearing some headline with the words *riot* and *Antichrist* in 72 point type. "Welcome to Dennington, City of Nutters." Dennington was suddenly a byword for medieval superstition. He had already told the press office to be "scathing" about the suggestion when responding to media calls and make comforting noises about not giving in to mob rule.

"He's late," the chief executive said. "Bet he's stopped off to survey the damage."

"Beelzebub?"

"No, Head of Housing. Are you alright?"

"Have you spoken to Audit about the stuff Graham Vance was downloading?"

"Yes."

"And?"

"It's pretty serious. Might be a good idea if he stood down from the Social Services sub-committee. And Audit thinks we should call in the police."

"Oh, *that* bad."

"Up to you, of course, Leader."

You could have made that decision yourself, Jeff thought. But it took a singularly brave chief exec to dump his political masters in the mire days before an election, and Lennie McAndrew was not that man. Nor was Graham Vance's taste in pornography the most pressing problem now.

The meeting was more bewildered than grim. While they discussed the cost of repairs and loopholes in tenancy conditions, nobody seemed keen to say the word. But Jeff felt he had to.

"How do we deal with the Antichrist angle?"

"I think we should just make a statement that we'll seek eviction of the rioters," said Lennie. "Antisocial behavior won't be tolerated etcetera etcetera. Dismiss it as mass hysteria and crack down hard."

Jeff looked at the Head of Housing. He shrugged. "Like it or not, these people are scared. They're threatening to do the bloke in Stanley Street now."

"Why?" said Jeff. "They've driven out two men they thought were the Antichrist. What are they claiming, mistaken identity?"

"Well, they're saying they were just his minions - "

"Oh, crap."

"Look, sir, I'm just reporting back. They now say the bloke in Stanley Street is the one. They want us to move him out. They're threatening to march on the town hall tomorrow."

"This is going to spread out of control if we don't find a way to take the heat out of the situation ."

"We could suggest he move out voluntarily, for his own safety."

"But he doesn't have to go."

"No. He doesn't have to do anything."

"Nothing we can evict him on? Is he in arrears with his rent?"

"He's done absolutely nothing, other than being the victim of someone pointing the finger. It's quiet up there this morning, but you hear groups of residents saying they know who the others are and that they're going to clear them all out if we don't act."

Nobody moved. Jeff looked round the table.

"Time for a reassuring visit," Jeff said. "Maybe Superintendent Davis would like to walk round Hursley Rise with me tomorrow. Before the worried citizens of the Rise give the media some handy photo opportunities on our doorstep." He gathered up his papers and headed for his office.

In the corridor, he ran into the chief internal auditor. The only thing he knew about her was that she liked to follow regulations. He always found it odd that a department whose name suggested number-crunching was actually an internal police force.

"Want to see me?" Jeff said.

"Just wondered if you had been made aware of the seriousness of the material Councilor Vance was accessing."

"I gather it's nasty."

"I'd say it's sufficient for him to be suspended from contact with vulnerable clients."

"Kids?"

"Any vulnerable group. We really need to let the police take a look at the downloaded files. You *are* going to refer it to them, aren't you?"

"As soon as I've got the Hursley Rise situation sorted," he promised, and he knew as soon as the words escaped him that he would find a reason not to.

Had it not been for a dozen TV news crews, a heavy police presence and scorch marks around the charred window frames of two boarded-up homes, Hursley Rise looked like any other working-class housing estate that morning. A bull terrier with a lavish studded collar was worrying a black plastic sack of rubbish left on the pavement. A man was up a ladder, painting his upstairs window frames a particularly vivid yellow. A workman was installing a satellite dish on the roof of the Duke of Buckingham.

"Houseproud area, in parts," said Superintendent Davis. She kept a definite distance from Jeff in the back seat of the police car. He could smell leather, spray starch and the same Chanel scent that Bev wore. "Not all thugs."

"More than half the residents here are ex-tenants who bought their own homes when we sold off council housing," he said. "Bet their property prices have fallen a bit overnight, eh?"

The officer didn't reply. The patrol car kept up a reasonable pace, slow enough for the two passengers to observe, but too fast to be a target for bricks. Near the row of shops by the bus stop, two constables were engaged in a conversation with a woman pushing a pram.

"Where did your lads say the march was going to assemble?"

"By the church."

St Peter and Paul was a redbrick church with a half-hearted bell tower and a peeling notice-board: if the forces of darkness were gathering here, it didn't look like God had his troops on the ground. On the tatty church green stood around a hundred women and a few men, most accompanied by children of varying ages who were showing signs of boredom. They had placards, held down like lances so that Jeff couldn't read the words, and two small boys were having a sword-fight with theirs.

"I can talk them out of this," Jeff said. Let me out here and I'll go and meet them."

Superintendent Davis looked unimpressed. "Wouldn't you like me there too?"

"Uniform might start them off again."

He thought he heard her stifle a snigger, but he said nothing and stepped out of the car into a chilly morning breeze. The twenty yards to the green suddenly seemed like a very long walk. He glanced back over his shoulder to check where the police car had parked.

As he got closer, some of the crowd turned to stare. A child with a placard was facing him, and he could pick out the words on her white tee-shirt: KILL EVIL NOW. And suddenly he recognized the woman beside her, with her bright red, dark-rooted hair and festoon of gold chain necklaces.

"Mrs. Avery," he said. "Are you the - leader of the deputation?"

She narrowed her eyes. There was a cigarette smoldering in her hand, held well away from her own child so that the smoke wafted towards someone else's.

"You come to talk to us now, have you?"

"If that's what you want." He was aware of people closing up behind him. Women and children or not, it was a neck-prickling sensation. "What can I say to reassure you?"

"Just get that bastard out. Or we'll be doing protest marches round the city until you do."

"You know I can't negotiate as long as there's the threat of violence."

Mrs. Avery flicked the growing ash from her stub. "A few hotheads. Can't blame people if they get frustrated. We told you them blokes was evil."

"You don't really believe there's an Antichrist, do you?"

She stepped a little closer. She was a head shorter than him and none the less terrifying for it. "You go and see him. It's the one next door to me. Stanley Street. The others was just his servants."

Jeff was going to suggest they invite the vicar to join the group to discuss the whole Antichrist concept when a thought hit him, a politician's thought. "Okay, Mrs. Avery," he said. "Do you know what I'm going to do now?"

"Amaze me."

"I'm going to walk down to Stanley Street and knock on his door and talk to..."

"Mr. Hobbs.

" . . .talk to Mr. Hobbs and show you he's just a lonely old man. A

mortal human. And maybe the kids are scared of him because he shouts at them when they're playing too near his garden. Doesn't that sound like a more rational explanation?"

Mrs. Avery had a half-smile on her face as she ground her cigarette out under a very high heel. She reached for her daughter's hand and pulled the child to her side. "Come on, Kayleigh, pick your placard up and keep behind the man." She gestured like a commissionaire at a posh hotel. "After you, Councilor Blake."

The worst that could happen, Jeff thought, was that the old boy would come out and threaten them with a walking stick. Then he could slip in and offer him a move to a nice new flat in the city center, with resident staff and a communal lounge area, and perhaps a cash incentive to help him settle in.

He kept walking, aware that Mrs. Avery was still behind him but at a slight distance. As they came into Stanley Street, she called out, "Number 27."

The two houses either side were relatively well-kept, one with window boxes of scarlet geraniums and one with a red and blue decorative cartwheel hanging on the front wall. But the grass in the small front gardens was blackened and shriveled along a foot-wide strip where it flanked the house in the middle.

Between them was a house that appeared not to be part of the street.

Jeff looked again. He looked up at the guttering and the line of the roof, and they ran smoothly into the next property. And yet it did not look *there*.

He put his hand on the gate. The wrought iron was polished, unrusted. The path to the door was immaculately-laid crazy paving, and there were no plants of any kind, not even the odd weed, just bare earth. He put up his hand to knock on the spotless battleship-gray paintwork.

The door swung open. A man in his late sixties stood there, ordinary as could be in gray corduroy trousers and a gray cardigan, smiling. He seemed to like gray a lot. It was then that Jeff felt the rush of cold air past him, as if he had opened a freezer door.

He looked round to say, "See, Mrs. Avery, he's just…" but she was too far away. A small crowd standing at stone-throwing distance was staring at the house, and they let loose a volley of bricks. One bounced off the window and hit Jeff in the leg before the old man grabbed his arm and pulled him into the hall to safety.

"You're Mr. Hobbs," he said. His leg stung. He glanced down at his trousers, baffled, and then realized the window was probably toughened double-glazing. "Lucky that didn't smash your window."

"No danger of that. I thought you might pop round, Councilor," said Hobbs. "Come and sit down."

The Antichrist's front parlor contained two gray velveteen chairs, a television and a plain pine sideboard. There were no photographs on the mantelpiece over the gas fire and no ornaments, except a carriage clock showing 10.23. Above it on the wall where most people might have hung a mirror was a framed sampler, embroidered as usual with an uplifting quotation; *All that is necessary for evil to triumph is that good men do nothing.*

Hobbs appeared in seconds with a tray bearing a pot and two porcelain cups of coffee. It smelled wonderful.

"Can't bear mugs," the old man said. "Got to have a drink out of a proper cup, eh, Councilor Blake?"

"Thank you." The coffee scalded his lips. "I imagine things have been quite hard for you this last few weeks, what with being here on your own and everything."

"Oh, the stones never touch the house. Don't worry about me."

"I feel pretty stupid having this conversation, actually." Hobbs seemed a pleasant old gent. "They think you're the Antichrist. Daft, isn't it? Wouldn't you like to move out for a while for your own safety? We can get you straight into a nice new flat. And we'd pay all your expenses, of course."

Hobbs sipped his coffee as if considering the offer. His face was unlined, and his eyes were clear, but all the same he still looked old. "I like it here," he said at last. "I don't have to move, do I?"

"We can't make you, Mr. Hobbs. You've done nothing. But we're worried about your safety, and we don't want any more rioting."

"Then I'll stay. I like it here."

"But it's not like you've been here all your life."

"Two months. But it feels like home."

"But -"

Hobbs held up a translucent and manicured hand to command silence, polite and firm, as if he had once been somebody important. "But I'm the

Antichrist, Councilor Blake. They can't harm me."

Oh boy, thought Jeff. *They're nuts, and so is he. Maybe he likes the attention. Maybe it stops him feeling so alone.* "Okay," he said carefully. "What if they come with the - er - local vicar and try to force you out with the power of God?"

For the first time Hobbs showed the faintest hint of annoyance and his forehead puckered slightly. "Now you're mocking me, Councilor Blake. Believe me, they're not wrong, and yet nobody listens to them."

Play along. Jeff snatched an idea out of memories of Sunday School. "If you're the Antichrist, why come to Hursley Rise? Why not the Middle East?"

"It's the atmosphere." Hobbs got up and inspected the coffee pot before topping up both cups. "No, there's plenty of raw material here for me."

"Evil?"

"Apathy, suspicion and cowardice. Would you call yourself a Christian, Councilor?"

"I suppose so."

"Then you probably think there's a little bit of God in all people. Personally, I think there's a little bit of *me* in everyone." He smiled engagingly, instantly a favorite uncle. "In political terms, I like to think of myself as the Opposition spokesman."

Jeff stared back at him for a while. He was, in every sense, the picture of harmless normality. Except for the young-old face, and the absence of all living things in the garden, and that cold, cold air. As Jeff stared, he could see his own breath forming wispy vapor in front of him and yet he didn't feel chilled. The clock now showed 11.15. Startled, Jeff bent his head automatically to drain his coffee cup, expecting to find it cold and the ideal cue to leave.

It scalded his mouth. He flinched.

"Still nice and hot," Hobbs said. "Shall I show you out?"

"Thank you." Jeff stood up and had to cast around him to find the door. "You'll think about what I said, though?"

"And you'll think about what I said." He smiled. "And don't worry too much about Graham Vance, will you?"

Jeff stopped, half-formed a question, and then thought better of it. He went to the window and rapped lightly on the pane with his knuckle. It was plain, ordinary, single-sheet glass - not toughened, not double-skinned. At that point he wanted to get out of the house more than anything he had ever wanted in his life.

The police car was waiting at a discreet distance. Superintendent Davis raised her eyebrows as if to ask what had happened.

"He won't go," Jeff said, shaking. "And shouldn't you have a copper outside his house or something?"

"Bricks never break his bloody windows," said the constable driving the car. It was the first time he had spoken. "None of us want to go near the place."

They drove off. Jeff locked his hands together to stop the shaking, meshing his fingers until they went white. And his lips still burned.

LETTERS TO THE EDITOR

Saturday April 28
Dear Sir,

Since Tuesday my life has been made a misery by these women parading up and down the streets with their children at all hours in a so-called peaceful protest. My car has been damaged and they have taken stones from my rock garden to throw at houses. I have lived at Hursley Rise for thirty years and I worked hard to buy my house to better myself. Now I could not sell it if I tried, thanks to this witch-hunt. Shame on the council for not putting a stop to it.

Yours faithfully
A respectable resident

WEDNESDAY, MAY 2

The chief executive's office overlooked the square and gave Jeff an excellent view of the protesters milling beneath them. On one side, Mrs. Avery's army of angry women trailed by toddlers was assembling; on the other, a smaller group of people milled around with placards bearing legends like LISTEN TO THE SILENT MAJORITY and LET US LIVE IN PEACE.

Mrs. Avery's troops waved placards a little less considered in their exhortations. Jeff could see at least one with BURN THEM OUT and a child sporting a tee-shirt labeled SATEN IS AMONG US.

"I think our education initiative in Hursley might have failed, judging by the spelling," said Lennie McAndrew, and munched a chocolate biscuit. Both men stood at the window and waited.

In the no-man's land between the factions, film crews and police drifted, stopping to interview in their own manner.

"You'd think the police would clear them out," Jeff said.

"A right to peaceful protest," said Lennie. "It's not as if they've done anything."

Jeff spotted Mrs. Avery giving an earnest interview to a TV reporter, waving her arm passionately in the direction of the town hall. A toddler she had been gripping by the hand wandered off unnoticed. The noise of the crowd, audible even with the windows closed, began growing from a hum into a tumult.

Something had clearly upset Mrs. Avery. She broke off from the interview and elbowed her way through the crowd to where a group of Concerned Residents Against Rioters had gathered.

She stopped in her tracks. Then she flung herself at a man in a red tracksuit and that was the last Jeff saw of her as the crowd began closing up, and fighting broke out.

"I was afraid this would happen." Police could be seen as small dark blue patches struggling in the crowd, salmon swimming against the current. "It's a police matter now, Jeff. Nothing we can do." The chief executive pulled the blinds. "Time you thought about the election."

"Right now, I'd rather not."

"About Graham Vance."

Jeff felt his heart sink. "What about him?"

"Either you or I have the power to refer the case to the police. I can understand why you might not want to do it before the election."

"I'd put it on the back-burner, to be honest."

"Bear in mind that once we start the process going, we have to inform Social Services because of the child protection angle. And after that we have very little control of it."

"What are you saying exactly?"

"You might want to delay this a while - say until the end of the year."

Jeff considered it. Yes, that would be far enough from this election and far ahead enough of the next for the political damage to be minimized.

But if Vance really was a risk to anyone, he had enough time to cover his tracks and continue whatever he might be doing.

Lennie seemed to interpret Jeff's silence as a prompt. "Or we could just sort it out internally. No fuss."

"Do nothing, you mean."

"Not exactly nothing - "

"You sound a lot like someone I was talking to yesterday," Jeff said, and he felt acid rise in his throat. "Maybe there really is a bit of Hobbs in us all."

Jeff went back to his own office and checked his messages. There were five threats of legal action from home-owners in Hursley Rise whose house sales had fallen through following the disturbances, and ten council tenants asking to be moved out of the area because they were afraid of reprisals.

It bothered Jeff that they called him rather than the housing department. That meant they identified him as the cause and solution to their crisis, and that boded ill for the polls on Thursday. The city was going to the dogs. And he was sure he could do nothing to stop it.

Police sirens wailed three storeys below. God only knew what the headlines would look like in the papers. Perhaps he could pull off something by lunchtime, something at the twelfth hour that would give him the front page in the evening paper. He decided to visit Mr. Hobbs one last time.

The Antichrist was sitting by the small fishpond in his back garden. There were neither fish in it nor plants: the surface was a frozen mirror. And there were no flowers or bushes in bloom, nor any starlings or blackbirds calling.

"I can't believe I'm having this conversation," Jeff said. The coffee was black, and still didn't seem to be cooling however long he left it. "But I'll ask again. Please, move out. Leave us alone and let these people try and heal their community."

Hobbs the Possible Antichrist nodded politely, a listening nod rather than an agreeing nod. "You believe them now, don't you?"

"Let's just say I've seen what you can do and the effect is the same whether you're who you say you are or

not. This neighborhood is destroyed. The buildings. Relationships. Trust. You've done it."

"I haven't done anything, Councilor Blake." Hobbs topped up his cup from the cheaply plated pot designed to look like chased silver. "I didn't have to. They did it all by themselves, and they started doing it the minute they didn't care where their kids were at night, or when they turned a blind eye to stolen goods, or even when they dumped their engine oil down the drain. That's why I didn't seek out war and unrest, Councilor. I can do my business best where people will do nothing, however small, to make things better."

"You create strife."

"It was always here."

"You've made damn sure they'll have something to fight over."

"As I said, councilor, I've done nothing. " He smiled, a really genuine smile. "Like you. You do *nothing* quite often, don't you? There's just the one of me. It took many more humans to bring this estate to its knees, and I couldn't have done it without them."

I am having a debate with the Antichrist. Jeff grasped at a fleeting feeling of amazement. All the party coups he had survived, all the secrets and favors he held against a political rainy day, were instantly dwarfed. He had no media audience, and yet he felt his sins were broadcast to the whole world.

The Antichrist's smile widened, as if he had shared Jeff's moment of revelation. "Graham Vance," he said. "Your own personal share of inaction,

among many. Good day, Councilor Blake."

When he walked back down Hobbs' path again, he noticed the dead patches of grass either side of Hobbs' fence had spread to swallow up both adjoining gardens.

It was still a pleasant spring day, even if he did have to dodge a petrol bomb lobbed by a couple of kids. Jeff left Hursley Rise dwindling in his rear view mirror. The further he drove from the riot zone, the more normal the world became. He counted the lilac trees: one, a gap, then twos and threes, and then a wall of blossom, and the scent that drifted in through the air vents was almost sickeningly sweet. He wondered how long it would be before they dried and shriveled, too.

He pulled into a garage to fill up. As he waited at the cash desk for his receipt, he glanced at the lunchtime edition of the local paper on the counter. ELECTIONS TOMORROW: WHO CAN SAVE THIS CITY? said the headline. "Not me," Jeff muttered, and the cashier glanced at him.

He pocketed his change and thought of Graham Vance. *You do nothing.* The taunt stung him. Nothing. And maybe he wasn't the man to save the city, either, but he had a growing feeling that there was one thing he could do, a small and selfless act that might start the world moving in another direction.

He took out his phone, thumbed through the directory and began dialing the Chief Internal Auditor.

While he listened to the ringing tone, he wondered if he should have called Graham and given him a sporting start. But political courtesies didn't matter any more. He waited, and looked back towards Hursley Rise, where there were surely others ready to cheat Hobbs out of the accumulation of small nothings upon which his victory hung.

"Audit?" he said. "I'd like you to call your vice squad contact, please. And make Councilor Vance's files available to them, will you?"

He was going to do something at last.

THE END

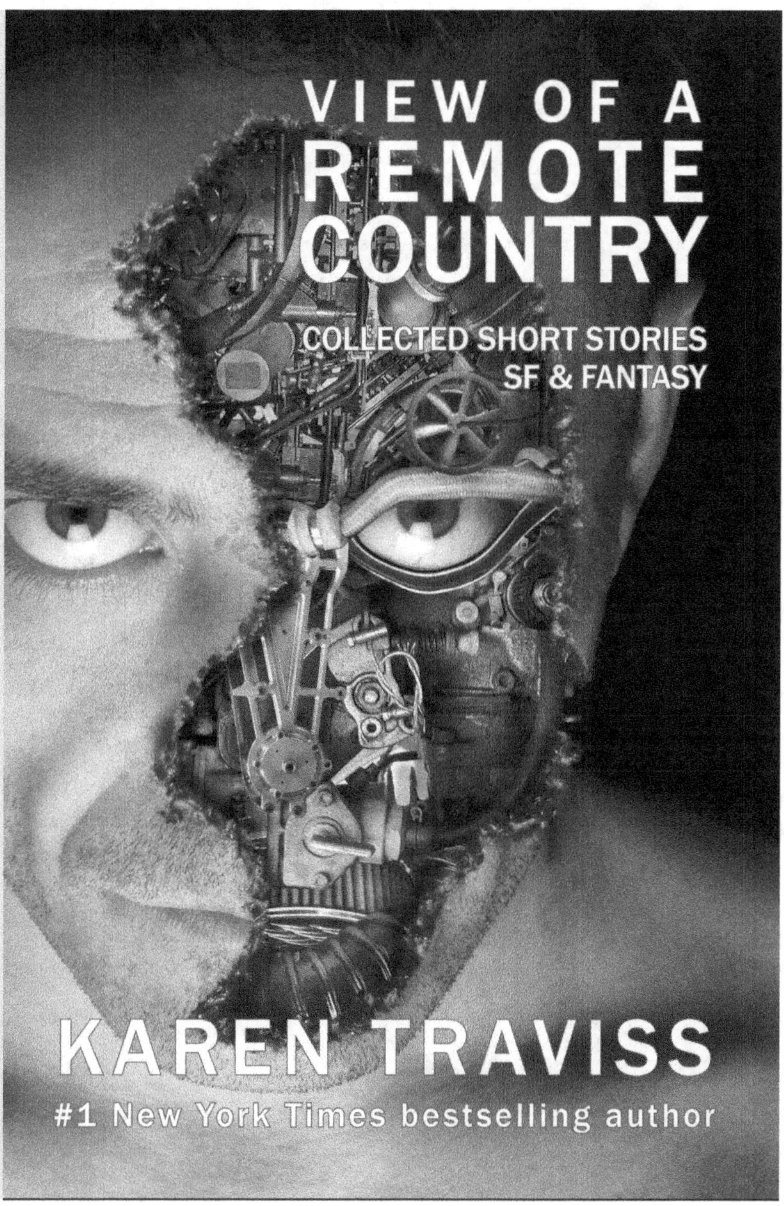

RICHARD CORY

Whenever Richard Cory went down town,
We people on the pavement looked at him:
He was a gentleman from sole to crown,
Clean favored, and imperially slim.

And he was always quietly arrayed,
And he was always human when he talked;
But still he fluttered pulses when he said,
"Good-morning," and he glittered when he walked.

And he was rich – yes, richer than a king –
And admirably schooled in every grace:
In fine, we thought that he was everything
To make us wish that we were in his place.

So on we worked, and waited for the light,
And went without the meat, and cursed the bread;
And Richard Cory, one calm summer night,
Went home and put a bullet through his head.

— Edwin Arlington Robinson
July 1897

STARCHILD

CYX HAD BEGUN TO FEAR THEY WOULD NEVER FIND A SUITABLE PLANET, THAT THEY WOULD SIMPLY DRIFT ENDLESSLY THROUGH SPACE UNTIL THE CHILD GREW OLD AND WITHERED AND... DIED.
NOW, AFTER SEVENTEEN YEARS, HIS SENSORS BEGAN TO BLINK AND THROB, IMPRINTING NECESSARY DATA ON HIS MEMORY BANKS. TIME TO TELEPATHICALLY STIR THE CHILD FROM UNTROUBLED DREAMS...
WRITTEN AND ILLUSTRATED BY BRUCE JONES

AWAKEN, CHILD-- WE WILL DESCEND UPON THE PLANET BELOW IN A FEW HOURS. AWAKEN AND REMEMBER ALL YOU HAVE BEEN TAUGHT. ACKNOWLEDGE...
I AM AWARE. OH, HOW LOVELY... ARE THESE... STARS?

GOOD. YOUR VOICE IS CLEAR, RESPONDING EXCELLENTLY. YES, THEY ARE STARS AND THIS IS SPACE. THE SPHERE BELOW IS A PLANET CAPABLE OF SUSTAINING YOU.
I SEE YOU NOW... THE SMALL METALIC CYLINDER. YOU ARE A CYXBRETNIC 7-400-G. I AM TO CALL YOU CYX. CORRECT?

EXCELLENT. . .YOUR RETENTION IS PERFECT. RECITE FOR ME WHILE WE DESCEND...

I AM A HUMAN FEMALE FROM EARTH AND AM 17 YEARS OLD.
I WAS CONCEIVED ABOARD THE STAR SHIP DORI ANN. ON NOV. 12, 3033 MY PARENTS AND CREW PERISHED IN A COSMIC STORM. I WAS BORN IN SPACE UP IN THE STAR BELT REGION OF THE NEILIAN GALAXY.
GOOD. NOW TELL ME ABOUT ME.
YOU ARE A COMPUTER ROBOT BUILT INTO THE DORI ANN TO FUNCTION AS CHEIF NAVIGATOR. YOU SURVIVED THE ACCIDENT OF NOV. 12...
...SALVAGED EQUIPMENT FROM THE WRECK, AND CONSTRUCTED A MEANS OF SELF-PROPULSION IN SPACE...
...YOU FOUND ME FLOATING IN SPACE, STILL ALIVE WITHIN MY MOTHER'S WOMB.
YOU ABORTED ME AND PROVIDED ME WITH LIFE SUPPORT.
WE ARE ENTERING ATMOSPHERE. YOUR HEAT RESISTANT PLACENTS AND UMBILICAL CORD ARE VISIBLE NOW AGAINST THE SKY.
LOOK CYX! LOOK AT THE COLORS!

YOU NOW HAVE WEIGHT. IT IS CALLED GRAVITY! YOU WEIGH 106 POUNDS.
YOU MUST LEARN TO WALK. REMEMBER WHAT I TAUGHT YOU.
CYX, LOOK! IT IS WONDERFUL!
COME. I WILL MANUFACTURE CLOTHING FOR YOU...
OH, THEY ARE BEAUTIFUL! I WANT TO WEAR THEM ALL AT ONCE!
DO YOU LIKE IT, CYX?
IT WILL SUFFICE. NOW YOU MUST HAVE FOOD AND SHELTER. THERE IS A POND NEAR BY. I WILL SHOW YOU HOW TO PURIFY THE WATER...
THERE IS A GIRL, CYX, LIVING IN THE WATER. SHE IS SMILING AT ME....!
CYX...!

IT IS A FORM OF REPTILE, I BELIEVE. I WILL TEACH YOU TO PREPARE AND COOK IT...
GRAPES! LOOK, CYX, I FOUND WILD GRAPES!
I SEE THEM. RUN CHILD... RUN AND BE FREE...
UM-M-M, I LIKE EATING, CYX. IT IS PLEASANT. I FEEL... I AM SO FULL...
SLEEP NOW, CHILD. I WILL WATCH AND TOMORROW WE WILL BUILD A SHELTER.
THEY ARE DELICIOUS! I LOVE THIS WORLD, CYX. IT IS BOUNTIFUL AND SWEET...
AND DANGEROUS, WERE YOU ALONE...
OH, YES, CYX. WITHOUT YOU I WOULD BE LOST! I OWE YOU SO MUCH... STAY WITH ME ALWAYS... NEVER LEAVE ME...
I WILL NOT LEAVE YOU, CHILD! COME, I WILL TEACH YOU MORE...

QUIETLY NOW... RAISE THE SPEAR... YOU ARE ALMOST WITHIN RANGE. DO NOT FRIGHTEN HIM...
GOOD THROW!
IT IS YOURS, CHILD... YOUR VERY OWN KILL. YOU DID IT YOURSELF!
BUT YOU TAUGHT ME, CYX.
YOU ARE CONTENT THEN, CHILD? YOU ARE NOT... LONELY?
LONELY?! WHAT IS THAT? I AM VERY HAPPY HERE. I HAVE THIS BEAUTIFUL WORLD...
...AND I HAVE YOU, CYX. TOMORROW WE CAN EXPLORE THE VALLEY BEYOND THE MOUNTAINS AND...
CYX! ARE YOU LISTENING TO ME?
I AM RECEIVING A SENSOR READING FROM THE SKY...
CYX, WHAT IS IT?
A SHIP... A STAR SHIP...

MAN HAS COME TO THE PLANET. GO TO HIM CHILD AND WELCOME HIM. DO NOT BE AFRAID...
I WILL BE WATCHING.

HE IS FROM EARTH, CYX. HIS NAME IS LEE AND HE LIVES IN A PLACE CALLED...CITY.

HE WISHES ME TO GO THERE WITH HIM.
IS IT IN YOUR MIND TO JOIN HIM? GO, THEN, I WILL REMAIN HERE.
BUT CYX...
IF EVER YOU SHOULD DESIRE TO RETURN, I WILL BE HERE.
GO NOW. THE EARTH MAN LOOKS IMPATIENT.

RUN, CHILD... RUN AND BE FREE...

THE SUMMER OF GRUNGE

BY JOHN GRAVES

I FOUND IT IN A BOX OF OLD COMIC books in my grandfather's attic: a near mint copy of *Detective Comics* No. 38. The cover featured Batman holding a paper-covered hoop, and Robin, billed as *The Sensational Character Find of 1940*, bursting through the paper. I knew as soon as I lifted it out of the box that it was valuable, and when I looked it up later, I was amazed.

It was the summer of Pearl Jam, the summer of *Nevermind*, the summer of grunge. My grandfather, my namesake Harlan Celley, died in July and my mother and I drove from our home in Carmel, Virginia up to New Hampshire for his funeral. He lived in a little town called Lancaster, population 1,859. My Mom told me the same anecdote about Lancaster on the drive up that I'd heard every summer since I was small. John Steinbeck, her favorite author, had visited the town while traveling cross-country with his dog. We read *The Pearl* in my English class the previous school year--I think we read it every year as matter of fact--and I had about as much interest in Steinbeck as I had in reading the dictionary. But she rambled on and I pretended to listen, watching the mountains towering all around us through the passenger window. I was seventeen.

Grandpa and I were as close as we could be living thirteen hours away. I loved him when I was a kid, but as the years piled on, as my interests shifted from the games boys play with their grandfathers to the games boys play with girls, we drifted apart. I saw him for a week every summer, and how well could two people know one another in such a short period of time?

The funeral was sober and small, with only me, my Mom and a handful of old yankees in attendance. My father was absent--he had not accompanied us to New Hampshire for a decade at least, and even the death of his father-in-law could not drag my Dad up to the North Country. Grandpa was laid to rest at the Summer Street Cemetery, and my Mom and I spent the next few days at his house on High Street. Mom was looking for letters and photo albums, things with sentimental value that would break her heart if they were stolen or pissed on by drunken teenagers. I was bored, my thoughts drifting continually southward toward my girlfriend, Amanda Mavis.

"Harlan," said my Mom, "why don't you go up into the attic and see if you can find anything interesting."

"Is that where Grandpa kept his *Playboys?*"

My mother smirked, which was about as close to laughter as she ever got. We both knew full well that Grandpa's *Playboys* were stored in one of the kitchen cabinets. I found them there, much to her chagrin, back when I was eleven. "I think he kept his collection of *Hustlers* up there," she said.

"Well, I guess I should liberate them from the dust bunnies."

It was good to see my Mom smile; she sure hadn't done it much as of late. She and Dad were fighting more often than not, and it seemed that my mother was slipping deeper into waves of despair. She came up for air every now and then, but after Grandpa was struck dead with a heart attack, I began to wonder if she would ever smile again.

THERE WAS WHAT APPEARED TO BE A closet on the second floor of my grandfather's house. Behind the door, however, was a staircase that led up to the attic. The wooden stairs were thick with dust, and my Converse high tops left distinct footprints on each step as I climbed to the top. There was no railing, and the hole in the attic floor was a safety hazard that would never pass a modern home inspection. But Grandpa's house was built around 1870, and things like personal safety didn't seem to matter so much back in those days.

There were several large pieces of furniture draped in white cloth up in the attic--don't ask me how they got them up those narrow stairs. I peeked under one cover, sending a volcanic cloud of dust into the air and revealing a green chaise lounge that boiled with silverfish. I found a rusty shotgun, a bunch of dime westerns, a near-complete collection of *Hardy Boys* novels and a yellowed box of the sort that people use to store magazines or comic books. Lifting off the lid, I knelt in the dust and flipped through the musty collection of periodicals.

Men of War. Have Gun Will Travel. The Rawhide Kid. There were some amazing comics in the box, and it was cool just to touch these four-color pieces of history. I'd stopped collecting comics when I was ten or eleven years old, but even I knew that I'd stumbled upon a treasure trove.

Then I flipped to the next issue in the box and nearly fainted. *Detective Comics* No. 38, and this issue was in beautiful condition. The pages were white, the cover free of folds and the staples held firm. I paged through the book, reading the tale of Dick Grayson, whose acrobat parents were murdered before his eyes.

"Holy shit," I whispered, realizing that the comic in my hands was worth a small fortune. I slipped *Detective* No. 38 between two issues of *All-Star Western* and bounded down the attic stairs. My Mom was in the kitchen, working on a cup of coffee, when I appeared in the doorway. "Find something interesting?" she asked.

"An old comic book. I think it might be worth some money."

She looked at me doubtfully. "Now you sound like your Uncle Billy."

"Huh?"

"My brother had hundreds of comics when we were kids. He was always trading them with his friends, convinced they were going to be worth a fortune someday. That's probably one of his."

"Do you think I could have it?"

She thought about it for a minute and then nodded. "Billy would have wanted you to have it. He..." Her words trailed off, and I knew why. Uncle Billy died in Vietnam when he was nineteen years old.

I could see the sorrow in my mother's eyes. She wanted to be left alone, to deal with her grief without me standing there watching her cry or scream or do whatever it was that she needed to do. "I was thinking about taking it over to the comic store," I said, "to see what it's worth."

"Is that really necessary?"

I shrugged my shoulders. "Probably not, but it'll get me out of the house for a few minutes. Can I take the car?"

She sighed, thought about it, and then dug into her purse. "Don't go anywhere but the comic store," she ordered. "Don't speed. Don't play the radio too loud."

"Yes, Ma'am."

She handed me the keys and a minute later I was behind the wheel of my mother's *Accord*. It wasn't great, but significantly better than my own car, a 1979 Mazda *GLC*. My car was what the kids in the *Hardy Boys* books would have called a jalopy. It was puke green, had no power steering and it sounded like an incoming torpedo when I rolled down the street. As I pulled out of my grandfather's driveway I was already imagining the awesome car I was going to buy myself when I sold *Detective* No. 38.

THE COMIC SHOP IN LANCASTER WAS unremarkable except for its complete disorganization. I browsed the store for fifteen minutes and finally had to ask the clerk to point me to the price guides. I took one off the shelf--it had Spider-Man on the cover--and flipped through the pages until I found *Detective Comics*. The entry read:

Good $1415.00...Fine $3550.00... Very Fine/Near Mint...$8500.00... Near Mint/Mint...$14,000.00.

Fourteen thousand dollars!

I approached the clerk, my hands trembling. He looked like a reject from an eighties hair band--mullet hair cut, stone-washed jeans, white Reeboks-- but I was too excited to pass judgment on a person that would have otherwise been a subject of my ridicule.

"Hey there," I said, "I was wondering if you buy old comics?"

He looked at me warily. "Sometimes. Depends on what you're selling."

"I have a copy of *Detective Comics* 38 in mint condition."

"Is it a reprint?"

"Nope. An original."

"Bullshit."

The scorn I had repressed only moments before rose up, and I was tempted to tell this asshole how I really felt about his stupid haircut, but I held back. "I have it my car," I said. "I can go get it."

"You do that," he said. "Let's see your comic so I can prove to you that it's a reprint."

Fuming, I stalked out of the store still holding the price guide. I returned a minute later with the comic, and as I handed it to Mullet-Man, I had a moment of terrible horror. I never bothered to check the publication date--it might very well be a reprint.

"Wow," he said after leafing through the first couple of pages. "This *is* the real thing."

"I told you so. Do you want to buy it?" I handed him the price guide, my finger marking the page that said I was about to be fourteen thousand dollars richer.

Mullet-Man took the guide and placed it on the counter, never even bothering to look at the page that I had marked. "I'll give you a hundred bucks," he said.

My face flushed. "One hundred? The guide says it's worth fourteen thousand."

"It's certainly not in mint condition..."

"But you just said..."

"And I have to be able to resell it." He considered the cover for a moment, nodded his head, and then turned back to me. "Tell you what, I'll give you five hundred."

"Screw this," I said. "I'll sell it in Virginia." I snatched the book from the counter and stormed out of the store.

The rest of my time in New Hampshire was uneventful, at least as far it pertains to this story. Mom and I went through my grandfather's house, collecting what few things we deemed important enough to drag back to Carmel. My mother was hoping to keep the house once the lawyers and bill collectors got their cut. "We can use it as a vacation home," she said, but I could tell by the tone in her voice that even she was doubtful.

We made the return drive on a Friday morning, and my Mom said that I should take the first leg. She figured that it would be safer to let me drive on the rural highways of New Hampshire rather than on I-95 where the trucks blow past you at 666 mph. We were in the southern part of the state, near Peterborough and Grovers Corners, when she stiffened and took in a sharp breath of air.

There was a giant moose standing on the side of the road. He was roughly the size of a school bus and about six yards from our car.

"Slow down," my mother shouted.

I complied, inching past the moose that just stared at us with glassy black eyes. If he stepped in front of our car we would have been totaled, but he never moved an inch. That was the only time I've ever seen a live moose, and to this day I've never forgotten the terror and the wonder.

THE FIRST THING I DID UPON MY return to Carmel was to pay a visit to Amanda. It wasn't too late, and I was hoping for some quality time, which is another way of saying time spent rolling around on her basement floor. We had been dating for almost a year at that point, and I'm ashamed to admit that I missed her more than my grandfather.

Amanda lived in a big house over in Carmel Heights, one of the best neighborhoods in town. I pulled into her driveway and parked behind her car, a red Ford *Probe* that her parents gave her for her sixteenth birthday back in January. The stars flickered upside down in her back window.

I approached the house and knocked lightly on the front door. It creaked open and James Mavis, Amanda's father, glared at me from inside their foyer.

"Harlan? What are you doing here?"

"I was hoping to see Amanda. Is she around?"

He nodded slowly, as if in deep concentration. After several moments, he spoke. "She's out with some friends. Went to the movies."

A harpoon of jealousy drove into my heart as he spoke, but I tried not to show it. "Do... you know... who she's with?" I asked.

Again that slow nod. "Some friends," he repeated.

"Well, can you... um, can you tell her that I stopped by? I'm back from New Hampshire."

He nodded and closed the door.

I would have texted Amanda if this has been ten years later, but teenagers didn't carry cell phones back in the days of grunge, and all I could do was wait. The minutes piled up as I circled around and around her neighborhood, navigating suburban side streets named for long-dead Confederate generals. Finally, I drove over to Carmel's comic book store, hoping for better luck than I'd had in Lancaster, but when I arrived the shop was closed for the night. There was, however, a poster for a comic convention hanging in the window. The show was slated for the following weekend.

This was it, my opportunity to sell *Detective* No. 38 for something resembling its true value. Maybe Amanda would even come to the show with me--it was less than an hour away in Tyson's Corner. Fantasies of the drive home, with fourteen thousand dollars in my pocket and Amanda on my lap, overwhelmed me. Still, I couldn't get past my jealousy that she was out with someone else instead of me.

I gave up eventually and returned home. I had to trust that Amanda was faithful; nothing she had done in our time together had ever indicated that she was not. I slept restlessly, with the phone beside my head and Pink Floyd's *The Final Cut* repeating on my boom box. I dreamt of my grandfather, of comic books, of first love.

★ ★ ★

AMANDA NEVER CALLED.

When I awoke the next morning, when I realized that I still hadn't heard from her, every fear you can imagine needled my heart. I fought off despair as the minutes ticked by until it was no longer too early to call.

"Good morning," I said, trying to disguise my concern about the night before.

There was silence for a few moments on the other end of the line, and then she spoke. "Hi, Harlan."

"I woke you up. I'm sorry." After what she put me through the night before, I wasn't really.

"It's fine," she said. "I'm glad you're back."

"I stopped by last night. You're Dad said you were out with friends."

"Lizzie and I saw *A League Of Their Own*. You would have hated it."

Elizabeth White was Amanda's best friend. The explanation seemed plausible enough, and I felt my fears deflating. Still, her father had mentioned *friends*-plural.

"How was your trip?" Her voice was mesmerizing, and I wanted more than anything to see her--to hold her.

"Lame. Well, mostly lame. I found something interesting in my grandfather's house."

"What's that?"

"And old comic book from the forties. It's worth about fourteen thousand dollars."

There was a long pause. "Whatever."

"Seriously. I bought a price guide and..."

"There's no way someone would pay that much for a stupid comic book," she said.

"A collector would. This is the first appearance of Robin. You know, Batman and Robin?"

"Of course I do."

"Anyway, there's a comic book convention up in Tyson's Corner next weekend. You want to go? We could sell this issue, buy me a new car, maybe make up for lost time."

She thought about it for so long that I wondered if she had drifted back to sleep. "Sure," she said at last. "That sounds like fun. Totally geeky, but this is *you* we're talking about."

"Thanks."

Our conversation settled into the banter of young lovers, and every trace of my previous fear and jealousy evaporated. Things were good with us, at least for a little while.

AMANDA DROVE WHEN WE WENT TO the comic convention the following Saturday. I'm not certain that my *GLC* would have made it there and back again, but I do know that Amanda was embarrassed to be seen in my P.O.S. car. She picked me up that morning and looked great in her Daisy Duke cutoffs and a tank top. She was wearing a pair of wayfarer sunglasses--I could see my own reflection every time I looked at her--and the kiss that we shared over the center console felt as sweet and as true as any I can recall.

We drove with the windows down, with the Red Hot Chili Peppers blasting on the stereo and our hands entwined. Life was good. We arrived at the convention, waited in line behind African-American Batman and Fat Supergirl, and finally made it to the showroom. I had *Detective* No. 38 stashed safely in my backpack and was in search of a comic dealer that could make me rich.

After exploring the room, we found a dealer that specialized in Golden Age comics. He was a heavyset man, ruddy-faced with thin-framed glasses and a five o'clock shadow. The banner over his stand read: Firebird Comics; Gary Sawyer, Proprietor. There were dozens of old books displayed on a wooden rack behind him, and at least a few had Batman on the cover.

The man seemed irritated as I approached, but when Amanda slunk up beside me it seemed that the dealer was willing to spare me at least a few moments of his time. "Mr. Sawyer?" I asked, "I was wondering if you buy old comics?"

"Depends? What've you got?" His eyes never drifted from Amanda as he spoke. She shifted under the weight of his gaze, pressing herself against my left arm.

I removed my bag from my shoulder, unzipped it, and withdrew my treasure. Sawyer's eyes shifted to the comic, to Amanda, and then back to the comic. "Holy shit," he whispered. "Let me see that."

He reached for *Detective* No. 38 and I handed it to him without thinking. "It's beautiful," he said, gently opening the cover and examining the pages. "How'd you come by this?"

"I found it in my grandfather's attic. There were some other books too... westerns and war comics."

He nodded, his attention as completely focused on the book as it had been on Amanda only seconds before. "That's real interesting, kid."

"I have a price guide. Says its worth, like, fourteen thousand dollars."

"That sounds about right," he said. "Probably more like twelve thousand, but you're in the right neighborhood."

Amanda and I turned to each other at the same moment, and I could see the excitement on her face.

"Twelve thousand," she mouthed.

I winked, feeling like a wheeler-dealer in an action movie. I had the girl, I was about to get the money and everything was coming up

roses. That meant, of course, that the shit was about to hit the fan.

"Are you offering me twelve thousand?" I was preparing to negotiate, hoping to haggle this guy up to thirteen.

He looked right at me and I could see evil in his eyes. He smiled slyly as he spoke. "Kid, I have no idea what you're talking about."

I looked at Amanda and then back at the dealer. "My comic. Are you going to buy it?"

"*Your* comic? This is an extremely rare book. I just don't think you can afford it."

"Dude, that's my comic. Why don't you just hand it over right now."

Sawyer tucked the book behind his back, and even though I was in the prime of life, there was no way I was going to be able to wrestle it away from him. Even if I could, the comic would probably be torn to scraps? "Kid, you just run along now," he said. "Don't make me call security."

"Security? What the fuck? Give me my god damned comic." Amanda's hand tensed around my arm for just a second, and then she let go.

"Little bastard," he muttered, and then his voice boomed throughout the convention hall. "Security! Security! I've got a thief here."

A crowd of geeky onlookers swarmed in, circling around us like fans at a professional wrestling match. I was Bret Hart, small and unlikely, and this five hundred pound douche bag was Yokozuna. I looked back over my shoulder, hoping Amanda might have some way out of this, but she was gone. I caught a glimpse of her as she blended into the throng; our eyes met for only a second and then she looked away.

"See, Kid," he said, "your girlfriend doesn't want to get in trouble. Why don't you run along before you get arrested?"

I spun on him so quickly, so ferociously, that Sawyer staggered backward. "That's mine," I said. "I found it in my grandfather's house. Now give it back."

I felt a strong hand on my shoulder and resisted the urge to throw an elbow. It's a good thing too, because I would have landed in quite a bit of trouble if I had. I turned to see a security guard standing behind me. He wore a brown uniform with sweat stains under his armpits and a pistol holstered on his utility belt. He had a gold nameplate under his badge that read: DILLS. "Young Man," he said, "what seems to be the problem here?"

"This guy stole my comic," I said.

"Don't listen to him," said the dealer. "He asked to see this book and then claimed it was his. Happens at every show." He shook his head in disgust.

Dills looked me up and down. "Is that true?"

"No. I found that comic in my grandfather's attic. I brought it here to try and sell it, and that... he took it to look it over and then wouldn't give it back."

The guard sighed and shook his own head. "One of you is lying," he said. He extended a hand toward Sawyer. "May I see the comic?" The dealer handed it over, and Dills' face lit up when he saw the cover. "Impressive. Is this the first appearance of Robin?"

"Yes," Sawyer and I said in unison.

Dills looked at me, his face deadly serious. "Young Man, I can see why you would want this comic book, but don't you think stealing is going a little too far?"

My whole body trembled with anger, but I managed to keep it contained. The last thing I needed was to mouth off to a rent-a-cop. "I wasn't trying to steal it," I said. "It's mine. If you ask..." I was going to tell him to ask Amanda, but she was long gone. I had never felt so betrayed, so alone in my life. "If you ask my mother, she'll tell you. We were up there last week for his funeral and..."

The guard stopped me with an outraised hand. "Don't say any more. Anything you say can and will be, you know?" He looked at Sawyer. "You wouldn't try to rip off a kid, would you?"

The dealer looked offended. "Of course not."

Dills stared at the comic in his hands, took a deep breath, and then looked at me. "I'd like you come down to my office," he said. "I'm going to have to call the police." His gaze shifted back to Sawyer, and I noticed beads of sweat on the large man's forehead.

"You're going to call the cops?" he asked.

"Afraid so."

Sawyer seemed to ponder this for a moment. "I don't know," he said. "I really don't want to press charges."

"That's your choice," Dills said. "But someone has to walk away with this comic."

The dealer stared at me, his eyes burning with hatred. "Listen, Kid, if I give you that book will you buzz off?"

"It's my book," I snapped.

"I'll take him down to my office," Dills said, "and see if we can work this out."

"But you won't call the cops?" Sawyer asked.

"I don't think that will be necessary."

"I hate to part with that comic, it's worth a lot of money, but there's no need for a kid to land in hot water with the cops."

"That's right," said Dills. "Come on, Young Man."

He lead me through the crowd and along a labyrinth of corridors into the bowels of the convention center. Dills never said a word the whole time, he just whistled quietly as we walked beneath sweating pipes and flickering florescent bulbs. We finally reached his office, a closet plastered with *Washington Redskins* merchandise, and he invited me inside. I sat in front of his desk, my head bowed and jaw clenched. How in the world did I wind up here?

"Son," he said, "I don't think you tried to steal that man's comic book."

I looked up, amazed. "You don't?"

Dills shook his head. "I remember that guy, he's pretty hard to forget. He tried something just like this about four years ago."

"Really?"

"Yeah. I had just started working here, and there was a big hoopla. As we looked into what happened, it turned out that Mr. Sawyer had a criminal record. And there were witnesses that backed up the real victim's story. Still, Sawyer insisted that the book was his

right up until the point when I suggested that we bring in the local police. After that, he was more than willing to let bygones be bygones. You know what I mean?"

"Yes, sir."

"Now, I'm going to ask you one last time, just to be sure. Is this your comic book?" He held out *Detective* No. 38.

"Yes, it is."

"And why were you trying to sell it?"

I thought about it for a minute. "I don't know. It's worth a lot of money, and my car is really a piece of, well, you know. I was hoping to use the money to buy a new car."

"Sports car?"

"Yeah."

"I was always partial to that Corvette Stingray myself. Never could afford one. You ever see one of those on the road?"

"I have."

"Well, they sure look pretty, but if it were me, I might hang on to a rare comic like this for a little while."

"Why?"

Dills shrugged. "You never know when you'll need the money for something really important."

We talked for a while longer, and then Mr. Dills let me go. I returned to the showroom, hoping to find Amanda, but she was nowhere in sight. I left the building, hiked across the parking lot to where we left her car, but she was gone. I had to call my Mom and ask her to come pick me up. As you can imagine, she was not happy.

MY STORY IS ALMOST DONE; THERE ARE just a few more things I have to say. I tried to call Amanda when I got home, but she didn't answer the phone. She avoided me for several days before finally confessing that it wasn't Elizabeth White with whom she went to the movies, but another guy.

"We've been together for so long," she said, "and I just need some space so I can figure out who I really am. You know?"

I knew. I can't blame her now, though I did at the time. We were different, Amanda and I, but I never knew it until she abandoned me at the comic convention. I would have never done that to her. Never. But time slips away and even old wounds heal eventually.

I didn't sell Detective No. 38 in 1992. I kept it in a box in my room, bagged and boarded, through four years of college, through my parents' divorce, through three apartments and an engagement. I got married in 2002 and considered selling the book to make the down payment on a house, but in the end I couldn't bring myself to do it. Mr. Dills' advice about waiting until I really needed the money kept tommyknocking around in my subconscious. I waited.

The year is 2012 as I write this. My mother died two months ago from Uterine Cancer. She spent most of the last twenty years living in my grandfather's house in New Hampshire. She was able to pay off the debts on the estate with her share of the divorce settlement. I promised to come visit regularly when she left, but the truth is that I only made it up to the North Country three or four times in twenty years. But I was with her at the end; I watched as she slowly lost the ability to eat, to speak, and even to stay awake. At 4:45 a.m. on January 29th, she stopped breathing. The silence was so eerie, and I'm not being dramatic when I say that I can hear it still.

I spent most of the following week at her house, at the house where this story began, going through her things. The doctors and the lawyers all wanted their cut, but they said I could remove the personal items, things with sentimental value that would break my heart if they were stolen or pissed on by drunken teenagers. Guess what I found up in the attic? The rest of my uncle's comics, old westerns and war stories that I hardly paid attention to back in 1992.

I sold the entire lot, including Detective Comics No. 38, just three days ago. I grossed over a hundred and twenty thousand dollars in all, more than enough to pay off the estate and keep my mother's house. Perhaps it will be a vacation home, a place where my wife and kids and I can come to remember the past and make new memories for the future. My Mom is gone; the boy that I was is gone, but I'll never forget the moose we saw driving back from New Hampshire one July morning so many years ago.

The past only dies if we allow ourselves to forget. If we hang on, if we endure, it can live forever.

THE END

Script: WOLFMAN • Art: ELDER

MEANWHILE, AT THE DOOR...
NOT BAD... NOT BAD AT ALL...
ALONE...NO ONE EVEN CLOSE BY! I CAN DO MY WORK UNDISTURBED!
AND THE ATMOSPHERE JUST REEKS OF THE GOTHOS OF OLD NEW ENGLAND...
LIKE SOMETHING OUT OF THE DARK SHADOWS...
NOOOO!
WHAA?
ARRGGHHHH!!
OTHERS COME ...TO DESTROY ME!
THE HEAVY BEAT OF FOOTSTEPS ECHOES DOWN THE LONG CORRIDOR AND DISAPPEARS SLOWLY IN THE STORMY NIGHT BETWEEN THE JAGGED FLASHES OF LIGHTNING AND THE CASCADING RHYTHM OF ENDLESS RAIN...
WILL LEAVE NOW...BUT WILL RETURN!
ARE YOU ALL RIGHT? ARE YOU?
UGGGHH WHAT IN THE WORLD HIT ME? FELT LIKE A BULL-DOZER!
THE LEGENDS OF NETHERCLIFT MANOR ARE MANY...SOME SAY THE BLOOD OF A HUNDRED MEN WERE SHED ONE DARK NIGHT. OTHERS INSIST THE ANCIENT MANOR WAS USED BY SATAN'S HORDES FOR THEIR WORSHIP OF THE DARK EVIL. AND STILL OTHERS TELL OF THE INHUMAN WAILING OF DYING BEASTS THAT COULD BE HEARD OVER THE COUNTRYSIDE THE MIDNIGHT OF EACH FULL MOON. ALL ARE PRESUMED TRUE!!!
I DON'T KNOW WHAT'S GOING ON HERE...BUT THAT THING WILL KILL THE GIRL IF I DON'T STOP IT!
THAT THING...WAS A MAN...ONCE... HE WAS MY FIANCE!
H...HE WAS WHAT?

WE WERE ELOPING...GOING TO GET MARRIED...BUT THEN I DECIDED NOT TO... IT WAS JUST ONE OF THOSE THINGS...I KNEW DEEP INSIDE ME, THAT I REALLY DIDN'T WANT TO MARRY HIM...
"I TOLD HIM TO TAKE ME BACK...THAT IT WAS OFF...BUT HE BECAME ANGERED...MAD! HE SAID IF HE DIDN'T HAVE ME, NO ONE WOULD!"
YOU'RE NOT LEAVING ME, CHERYSE...EVER!
I'M NOT GOING TO ARGUE WITH YOU, UNDERSTAND ME?
BRIDGE OUT DANGER!
BUT I DON'T LOVE YOU... I CAN'T MARRY YOU!
I'LL HURT YOU SO MUCH NO MAN WILL EVER WANT TO EVEN LOOK AT YOU!
I'LL HURT YOU PLENTY BEFORE I LET YOU GO!
LEAVE ME GO... YOU'RE HURTING ME!
"WE KEPT ON STRUGGLING, AND THEN THE ROAD STOPPED, AND THE CAR WENT FLYING INTO THE AIR! SOMEHOW I FELL OUT BEFORE THE CAR CRASHED! BUT EVEN AS IT WENT UNDER, I COULD HEAR HIM SCREAMING...CURSING...
"HE WOULDN'T LET ME OUT. I TRIED, BUT HE GRABBED MY HAND AND FORCED ME BACK INTO THE CAR. HE HURT ME SO MUCH I WANTED TO SCREAM."
I'LL GET YOU, CHERYSE... I'LL KILL YOU...KILL YOU... AYYYAAAGGHH!
STOP
IT WAS POURING, AND THIS WAS THE ONLY PLACE AROUND. I CAME HERE... TIRED...HALF DEAD, AND FOR TWO DAYS WAITED FOR THE RAIN TO STOP OR FOR SOMEONE TO FIND ME...
AWOOOOOO!!
SOMEONE DID...
WHAT WAS THAT SOUND? IT WAS LIKE A HEART WAILING IN THE NIGHT!
MY FIANCE... PAUL...THE CREATURE!
TWO DAYS AFTER THE ACCIDENT THERE WAS A POUNDING AT THE DOOR. I THOUGHT SOMEONE WAS COMING TO SAVE ME BUT IT WAS PAUL, COME BACK FROM THE GRAVE ...HIDEOUS... DISFIGURED...
AND OUT TO KILL ME! THAT WAILING SOUND MEANS HE IS GOING TO TRY AGAIN!

THE LIGHTS... THEY'RE OUT!
HE MUST'VE CUT THE WIRES... PUT US IN THE DARK... WE'LL NEED THE CANDLE FOR LIGHT...
THAT AND GETTING OUT OF THIS MAD HOUSE. C'MON!
I WANTED TO GET AWAY FROM PEOPLE... TO BE ALONE TO DO MY WRITING. BUT AFTER THIS I'M GONNA STAY RIGHT IN THE MIDDLE OF EVERYTHING. I'M NOT GONNA CATCH ME ALONE EVER AGAIN!
ARRGGHHH!! I GET YOU NOW, CHERYSE... YOU KILL NO MORE!
WATCH OUT... IT'S GONNA LEAP!
ARRGGHHH!!
YAAAGGHHHHH!
SHE LIED... LIED... SHE KILLS... RUN... RUN... BEFORE IT IS TOO LATE... TOO LATE...

WHAT DID HE MEAN BY THAT? WHY DID HE SAY YOU KILLED HIM?
I TOLD YOU...HE BLAMES ME FOR HIS DEATH...HE THINKS THAT I KILLED HIM...
HE'S JUST CRAZY...YOU DON'T WANT TO LISTEN TO HIM NOW, DO YOU? NOW THAT WE'RE ALONE...TOGETHER.
GIVE ME A KISS, MY HERO...KISS ME!
YOUR LIPS...THEY'RE LIKE ICE...LIKE DEATH ITSELF!
YOU'RE JUST LIKE HIM...YOU CAN SENSE IT, CAN'T YOU?
I LOST HIM BECAUSE I WAS CARELESS...BUT WON'T LOSE YOU, MY DEAR...
I WON'T LOSE YOU, BECAUSE I NEED YOU!
DON'T STRUGGLE...BECAUSE IT WILL DO YOU NO GOOD...IT NEVER DOES. I'M FAR STRONGER THAN YOU!
THE OTHER WAS A FOOL...I WANTED HIS LIFE FORCE SO I COULD LIVE...
BUT HE STRUGGLED AND LOOK WHAT HAPPENED TO HIM!
I'M A SUCCUBUS...I NEED YOUR LIFE...YOUR ENERGY TO KEEP ME ALIVE...I MUST HAVE YOUR KISSES...I MUST!
LET ME HAVE YOUR ENERGY...YOU MUST! I'M DYING...PAUL FOUGHT WHEN HE DISCOVERED WHAT I WAS...I COULDN'T CONTROL THE WAY I TOOK HIS LIFE FORCE, AND HE TURNED INTO THAT THING! PLEASE DON'T LET ME DO THAT TO YOU...I NEED YOUR LIFE...IT'S EITHER YOU OR ME...
DON'T YOU UNDERSTAND...IT'S EITHER...AGGGHHH!!
NO, CHERYSE...YOU KILLED TOO MUCH ALREADY...YOU WON'T KILL AGAIN...EVER...
MMMFFFFF!!!
THE STORM REACHES OUT WITH FREEZING FINGERS AND THE DUST THAT ONCE WAS CHERYSE IS SCATTERED TO THE WIND. AND YOU RUN FROM THE HOUSE OF MADNESS, ENTER YOUR CAR, AND BECOME TERRIBLY, TERRIBLY ILL...
The End

OZYMANDIAS

I met a traveller from an antique land
Who said: Two vast and trunkless legs of stone
Stand in the desart. Near them, on the sand,
Half sunk, a shattered visage lies, whose frown,
And wrinkled lip, and sneer of cold command,
Tell that its sculptor well those passions read
Which yet survive, stamped on these lifeless things,
The hand that mocked them and the heart that fed:
And on the pedestal these words appear:
"My name is Ozymandias, King of Kings:
Look on my works, ye Mighty, and despair!"
No thing beside remains. Round the decay
Of that colossal wreck, boundless and bare
The lone and level sands stretch far away.

— Percy Bysshe Shelley
January 1818

THE BRIDGE OF SAN LUIS REY

BY THORNTON WILDER

PART FOUR:
UNCLE PIO

IN ONE OF HER LETTERS (THE XXIXth) the Marquesa de Montemayor tries to describe the impression that Uncle Pio *"our aged Harlequin"* made upon her: *"I have been sitting all morning on the green balcony making you a pair of slippers, my soul,"* she tells her daughter. *"As the golden wire did not take up my whole attention I was able to follow the activity of a coterie of ants in the wall beside me. Somewhere behind the partition they were patiently destroying my house. Every three minutes a little workman would appear between two boards and drop a grain of wood upon the floor below. Then he would wave his antennae at me and back busily into his mysterious corridor. In the meantime various brothers and sisters of his were trotting back and forth on a certain highway, stopping to massage one another's heads, or if the messages they bore were of first importance, refusing angrily to massage or to be massaged. And at once I thought of Uncle Pio. Why? Where else but with him had I seen that very gesture with which he arrests a passing abbé or a courtier's valet, and whispers, his lips laid against his victim's ear? And surely enough, before noon I saw him hurry by on one of those mysterious errands of his. As I am the idlest and silliest of women I sent Pepita to get me a piece of nougat which I placed on the ant's highway. Similarly I sent word to the Café Pizarro asking them to send Uncle Pio to see me if he dropped in before sunset. I shall give him that old bent salad fork with the turquoise in it, and he will bring me a copy of the new ballad that everyone is singing about the d—q—a of Ol—v—s. My child, you shall have the best of everything, and you shall have it first."*

And in the next letter: *"My dear, Uncle Pio is the most delightful man in the world, your husband excepted. He is the second most delightful man in the world. His conversation is enchanting. If he weren't so disreputable I should make him my secretary. He could write all my letters for me and generations would rise up and call me witty. Alas, however, he is so moth-eaten by disease and bad company, that I shall have to leave him to his underworld. He is not only like an ant, he is like a soiled pack of cards. And I doubt whether the whole Pacific could wash him sweet and fragrant again. But what divine Spanish he speaks and what exquisite things he says in it! That's what one gets by hanging around a theatre and hearing nothing but the conversation of Calderón. Alas, what is the matter with this world, my soul, that it should treat such a being so ill! His eyes are as sad as those of a cow that has been separated from its tenth calf."*

YOU SHOULD KNOW FIRST THAT THIS Uncle Pio was Camila Perichole's maid. He was also her singing-master, her coiffeur, her masseur, her reader, her errand-boy, her banker; rumor added: her father. For example, he taught her her parts. There was a whisper around town that Camila could read and write. The compliment was unfounded; Uncle Pio did her reading and writing for her. At the height of the season the company put on two or three new plays a week, and as each one contained a long and flowery part for the Perichole the mere task of memorization was not a trifle.

Peru had passed within fifty years from a frontier state to a state in renaissance. Its interest in music and the theatre was intense. Lima celebrated its feast days by hearing a Mass of Tomás Luis da Victoria in the morning and the glittering poetry of Calderón in the evening. It is true that the Limeans were given to interpolating trivial songs into the most exquisite comedies and some lachrymose effects into the austerest music; but at least they never submitted to the boredom of a misplaced veneration. If they had

disliked heroic comedy the Limeans would not have hesitated to remain at home; and if they had been deaf to polyphony nothing would have prevented their going to an earlier service. When the Archbishop returned from a short trip to Spain, all Lima kept asking: "What has he brought?" The news finally spread abroad that he had returned with tomes of masses and motets by Palestrina, Morales I and Vittoria, as well as thirty-five plays by Tirso de Molina and Ruiz de Alarçon and Moreto. There was a civic fête in his honor. The choirboys' school and the green room of the Comedia were swamped with the gifts of vegetables and wheat. All the world was eager to nourish the interpreters of so much beauty.

This was the theatre in which Camila Perichole gradually made her reputation. So rich was the repertory and so dependable the prompter's box that few plays were given more than four times a season. The manager had the whole flowering of the 17th Century Spanish drama to draw upon, including many that are now lost to us. The Perichole had appeared in a hundred plays of Lope de Vega alone. There were many admirable actresses in Lima during these years, but none better. The citizens were too far away from the theatres of Spain to realize that she was the best in the Spanish world. They kept sighing for a glimpse of the stars of Madrid whom they had never seen and to whom they assigned vague new excellences. Only one person knew for certain that the Perichole was a great performer and that was her tutor Uncle Pio.

Uncle Pio came of a good Castilian house, illegitimately. At the age of ten he ran away to Madrid from his father's hacienda and was pursued without diligence. He lived ever after by his wits. He possessed the six attributes of the adventurer—a memory for names and faces, with the aptitude for altering his own; the gift of tongues; inexhaustible invention; secrecy; the talent for falling into conversation with strangers; and that freedom from conscience that springs from a contempt for the dozing rich he preyed upon. From ten to fifteen he distributed handbills for merchants, held horses, and ran confidential errands. From fifteen to twenty he trained bears and snakes for travelling circuses; he cooked, and mixed punches; he hung about the entries of the more expensive taverns and whispered informations into the travellers' ears—sometimes nothing more dubious than that a certain noble house was reduced to selling its plate and could thus dispense with the commission of a silversmith. He was attached to all the theatres in town and could applaud like ten. He spread slanders at so much a slander. He sold rumors about crops and about the value of land. From twenty to thirty his services came to be recognized in very high circles—he was sent out by the government to inspirit some half-hearted rebellions in the mountains, so that the government could presently arrive and whole-heartedly crush them. His discretion was so profound that the French party used him even when they knew that the Austrian party used him also. He had long interviews with the Princesse des Ursins, but he came and went by the back stairs. During this phase he was no longer obliged to arrange gentlemen's pleasures, nor to plant little harvests of calumny.

He never did one thing for more than two weeks at a time even when enormous gains seemed likely to follow upon it. He could have become a circus manager, a theatrical director, a dealer in antiquities, an importer of Italian silks, a secretary in the Palace or the Cathedral, a dealer in provisions for the army, a speculator in houses and farms, a merchant in dissipations and pleasures. But there seemed to have been written into his personality, through some accident or early admiration of his childhood, a reluctance to own anything, to be tied down, to be held to a long engagement. It was this that prevented his thieving, for example. He had stolen several times, but the gains had not been sufficient to offset his dread of being locked up; he had sufficient ingenuity to escape on the field itself all the police in the world, but nothing could protect him against the talebearing of his enemies. Similarly he had been reduced for a time to making investigations for the Inquisition, but when he had seen several of his victims led off in hoods he felt that he might be involving himself in an institution whose movements were not evenly predictable.

As he approached twenty, Uncle Pio came to see quite clearly that his life had three aims. There was first this need of independence, cast into a curious pattern, namely: the desire to be varied, secret and omniscient. He was willing to renounce the dignities of public life, if in secret he might feel that he looked down upon men from a great distance, knowing more about them than they knew themselves; and with a knowledge which occasionally passed into action and rendered him an agent in the affairs of states and persons. In the second place he wanted to be always near beautiful women, of whom he was always in the best and worst sense the worshipper. To be near them was as necessary to him as breathing. His reverence for beauty and charm was there for anyone to see and to laugh at, and the ladies of the theatre and the court and the houses of pleasure loved his connoisseurship. They tormented him and insulted him and asked his advice and were singularly comforted by his absurd devotion. He suffered greatly their rages and their meannesses and their confiding tears; all he asked was to be accepted casually, to be trusted, to be allowed like a friendly and slightly foolish dog to come and go in their rooms and to write their letters for them. He was insatiably curious about their minds and their hearts. He never expected to be loved by them (borrowing for a moment another sense of that word); for that, he carried his money to the obscurer parts of the city; he was always desperately unprepossessing, with his whisp of a moustache and his whisp of a beard and his big ridiculous sad eyes. They constituted his parish; it was from them that he acquired the name of Uncle Pio and it was when they were in trouble that he most revealed himself; when they fell from favour he lent them money, when they were ill he outlasted the

flagging devotion of their lovers and the exasperation of their maids; when time or disease robbed them of their beauty, he served them still for their beauty's memory; and when they died his was the honest grief that saw them as far as possible on their journey.

In the third place he wanted to be near those that loved Spanish literature and its masterpieces, especially in the theatre. He had discovered all that treasure for himself, borrowing or stealing from the libraries of his patrons, feeding himself upon it in secrecy,—behind the scenes, as it were, of his mad life. He was contemptuous of the great persons who for all their education and usage, exhibited no care nor astonishment before the miracles of word order in Calderón and Cervantes. He longed himself to make verses. He never realized that many of the satirical songs he had written for the vaudevilles passed into folk-music and have been borne everywhere along the highroads.

As the result of one of those quarrels that arise so naturally in brothels his life became too complicated and he removed to Peru. Uncle Pio in Peru was even more versatile than Uncle Pio in Europe. Here too he touched upon real-estate, circuses, pleasures, insurrections and antiques. A Chinese junk had been blown from Canton to America; he dragged up the beach the bales of deep-red porcelain and sold the bowls to the collectors of virtú. He traced down the sovereign remedies of the Incas and started a smart trade in pills. Within four months he knew practically everyone in Lima. He presently added to this acquaintance the inhabitants of scores of seacoast towns, mining camps and settlements in the interior. His pretensions to omniscience became more and more plausible. The Viceroy discovered Uncle Pio and all this richness of reference; he engaged his services in many affairs. In the decay of his judgment Don Andrés had retained one talent, he was a master of the technique of handling confidential servants. He treated Uncle Pio with great tact and some deference; he understood which errands the other should not be asked to undertake and he understood his need for variety and intermission. Uncle Pio in turn was perpetually astonished that a prince should make so little use of his position, for power, or for fantasy, or for sheer delight in the manipulation of other men's destinies; but the servant loved the master because he could quote from any of Cervantes' prefaces and because his tongue had a little Castilian salt about it still. Many a morning Uncle Pio entered the Palace through corridors where there was no one to cross but a confessor or a confidential bully and sat with the Viceroy over his morning chocolate.

But for all his activity nothing made Uncle Pio rich. One would have said that he abandoned a venture when it threatened to prosper. Although no one knew it, he owned a house. It was full of dogs that could add and multiply and the top floor was reserved for birds. But even in this kingdom he was lonely, and proud in his loneliness, as though there resided a certain superiority in such a solitude. Finally he stumbled upon an adventure that came like some strange gift from the skies and that combined the three great aims of his life: his passion for overseeing the lives of others, his worship of beautiful women, and his admiration for the treasures of Spanish literature. He discovered Camila Perichole. Her real name was Micaela Villegas. She was singing in cafés at the age of twelve and Uncle Pio had always been the very soul of cafés. Now as he sat among the guitarists and watched this awkward girl singing ballads, imitating every inflection of the more experienced singers who had preceded her, the determination entered his mind to play Pygmalion. He bought her. Instead of sleeping locked up in the wine bin, she inherited a cot in his house. He wrote songs for her, he taught her how to listen to the quality of her tone, and bought her a new dress. At first all she noticed was that it was wonderful not to be whipped, to be offered hot soups, and to betaught something. But it was Uncle Pio who was really dazzled. His rash experiment flourished beyond all prophecy. The little twelve-year-old, silent and always a little sullen, devoured work. He set her endless exercises in acting and mimicry; he set her problems in conveying the atmosphere of a song; he took her to the theatres and made her notice all the details of a performance. But it was from Camila as a woman that he was to receive his greatest shock. The long arms and legs were finally harmonized into a body of perfect grace. The almost grotesque and hungry face became beautiful. Her whole nature became gentle and mysterious and oddly wise; and it all turned to him. She could find no fault in him and she was sturdily loyal. They loved one another deeply but without passion. He resected the slight nervous shadow that crossed her face when he came too near her. But there arose out of this denial itself the perfume of a tenderness, that ghost of passion which, in the most unexpected relationship, can make even a whole lifetime devoted to irksome duty pass like a gracious dream.

They travelled a great deal, seeking new taverns, for the highest attribute of a café singer will always be her novelty. They went to Mexico, their odd clothes wrapped up in the self-same shawl. They slept on beaches, they were whipped at Panama and shipwrecked on some tiny Pacific islands plastered with the droppings of birds. They tramped through jungles delicately picking their way among snakes and beetles. They sold themselves out as harvesters in a hard season. Nothing in the world was very surprising to them.

Then began an even harder course of training for the girl, a regimen that resembled more the preparation for an acrobat. The instruction was a little complicated by the fact that her rise to favor was very rapid; and there was some danger that the applause she received would make her content with her work too soon. Uncle Pio never exactly beat her, but he resorted to a sarcasm that had terrors of its own.

At the close of a performance Camila would return to her dressing room to find Uncle Pio whistling nonchalantly in one corner. She would divine his attitude at once and cry angrily:

"Now what is it? Mother of God, Mother of God, what is it now?"

"Nothing, little pearl. My little Camila of Camilas, nothing."

"There was something you didn't like. Ugly fault-finding thing that you are. Come on now, what was it? Look, I'm ready."

"No, little fish. Adorable morning star, I suppose you did as well as you could."

The suggestion that she was a limited artist and that certain felicities would be forever closed to her never failed to make Camila frantic. She would burst into tears: "I wish I had never known you. You poison my whole life. You just think I did badly. It pleases you to pretend that I was bad. All right then, be quiet."

Uncle Pio went on whistling.

"The fact is I know I was weak to-night, and don't need you to tell me so. So there. Now go away. I don't want to see you around. It's hard enough to play that part without coming back and finding you this way."

Suddenly Uncle Pio would lean forward and ask with angry intensity: "Why did you take that speech to the prisoner so fast?"

More tears from the Perichole: "Oh God, let me die in peace! One day you tell me to go faster and another to go slower. Anyway I shall be crazy in a year or two and then it won't matter."

More whistling.

"Besides the audience applauded as never before. Do you hear me? *As never before*. There! Too fast or too slow is nothing to them. They wept.

I was divine. That's all I care for. Now be silent. Be silent."

He was absolutely silent.

"You may comb my hair, but if you say another word I shall never play again. You can find some other girl, that's all."

Thereupon he would comb her hair soothingly for ten minutes, pretending not to notice the sobs that were shaking her exhausted body. At last she would turn quickly and catching one of his hands would kiss it frantically: "Uncle Pio, was I so bad? Was I a disgrace to you? Was it so awful *that you left the theatre?*"

After a long pause Uncle Pio would admit judiciously: "You were good in the scene on the ship."

"But I've been better, Uncle Pio. You remember the night you came back from Cuzco——?"

"You were pretty good at the close."

"Was I?"

"But my flower, my pearl, *was the matter in the speech to the prisoner?*"

Here the Perichole would fling her face and arms upon the table amid the pomades, caught up into a tremendous fit of weeping. Only perfection would do, only perfection. And that had never come.

Then beginning in a low voice Uncle Pio would talk for an hour, analyzing the play, entering into a world of finesse in matters of voice and gesture and tempo, and often until dawn they would remain there declaiming to one another the lordly conversation of Calderón.

Whom were these two seeking to please? Not the audiences of Lima.

They had long since been satisfied. We come from a world where we have known incredible standards of excellence, and we dimly remember beauties which we have not seized again; and we go back to that world. Uncle Pio and Camila Perichole were tormenting themselves in an effort to establish in Peru the standards of the theatres in some Heaven whither Calderón had preceded them. The public for which masterpieces are intended is not on this earth.

With the passing of time Camila lost some of this absorption in her art. A certain intermittent contempt for acting made her negligent. It was due to the poverty of interest in women's rôles throughout Spanish classical drama. At a time when the playwrights grouped about the courts of England and France (a little later, of Venice) were enriching the parts of women with studies in wit, charm, passion and hysteria, the dramatists of Spain kept their eyes on their heroes, on gentlemen torn between the conflicting claims of honour, or, as sinners, returning at the last moment to the cross. For a number of years Uncle Pio spent himself in discovering ways to interest the Perichole in the rôles that fell to her. Upon one occasion he was able to announce to Camila that a granddaughter of Vico de Barrera had arrived in Peru. Uncle Pio had long since communicated to Camila his veneration for great poets and Camila never questioned the view that they were a little above the kings and not below the saints. So it was in great excitement that the two of them chose one of the master's plays to perform before his granddaughter. They rehearsed the poem a hundred times, now in the great joy of invention, now in dejection. On the night of the performance Camila peering out between the folds of the curtain had Uncle Pio point out to her the little middle-aged woman worn with the cares of penury and a large family; but it seemed to Camila that she was looking at all the beauty and dignity in the world. As she waited for the lines that preceded her entrance she clung to Uncle Pio in reverent silence, her heart beating loudly. Between the acts she retired to the dusty corner of the warehouse where no one would find her and sat staring into the corners. At the close of the performance Uncle Pio brought the granddaughter of Vico de Barrera into Camila's room. Camila stood among the clothes that hung upon the wall, weeping with happiness and shame. Finally she flung herself on her knees and kissed the older woman's hands, and the older woman kissed hers, and while the audience went home and went to bed the Visitor remained telling Camila the little stories that had remained in the family, of Vico's work and of his habits.

Uncle Pio was at his happiest when a new actress entered the company, for the discovery of a new talent at her side never failed to bestir the Perichole. To Uncle Pio (standing at the back of the auditorium, bent double with joy and malice) it seemed that the body of the Perichole had become an alabaster lamp in which a strong light had been placed. Without any resort to tricks or to false emphasis, she set herself to efface the newcomer.

If the play were a comedy she became the very abstraction of wit, and (as was more likely) it was a drama of wronged ladies and implacable hates, the stage fairly smouldered with her emotion. Her personality became so electric that if she so much as laid her hand upon that of a fellow actor a sympathetic shudder ran through the audience. But such occasions of excellence became less and less frequent. As her technique became sounder, Camila's sincerity became less necessary. Even when she was absentminded the audience did not notice the difference and only Uncle Pio grieved.

Camila had a very beautiful face, or rather a face beautiful save in repose. In repose one was startled to discover that the nose was long and thin, the mouth tired and a little childish, the eyes unsatisfied—a rather pinched peasant girl, dragged from the cafés-chantants and quite incapable of establishing any harmony between the claims of her art, of her appetites, of her dreams, and of her crowded daily routine. Each of these was a world in itself, and the warfare between them would soon have reduced to idiocy (or triviality) a less tenacious physique. We have seen that in spite of her discontent with her parts, the Perichole knew very well the joy that might reside in acting and warmed herself from time to time at that flame. But that of love attracted her more often, though with no greater assurance of happiness, until Jupiter himself sent her some pearls.

Don Andrés de Ribera, the Viceroy of Peru, was the remnant of a delightful man, broken by the table, the alcove, a grandeeship and ten years of exile. As a youth he had accompanied embassies to Versailles and Rome; he had fought in the wars in Austria; he had been in Jerusalem. He was a widower and childless of an enormous and wealthy woman; he had collected coins a little, wines, actresses, orders and maps. From the table he had received the gout; from the alcove a tendency to convulsions; from the grandeeship a pride so vast and puerile that he seldom heard anything that was said to him and talked to the ceiling in a perpetual monologue; from the exile, oceans of boredom, a boredom so persuasive that it was like pain,—he woke up with it and spent the day with it, and it sat by his bed all night watching his sleep. Camila was passing the years in the hard-working routine of the theatre, savoured by a few untidy love-affairs, when this Olympian personage (for he had a face and port fit to play gods and heroes on the scene) suddenly transported her to the most delicious midnight suppers at the Palace. Contrary to all the traditions of the stage and state she adored her elderly admirer; she thought she was going to be happy forever. Don Andrés taught the Perichole a great many things and to her bright eager mind that was one of the sweetest ingredients of love. He taught her a little French; to be neat and clean; the modes of address. Uncle Pio had taught her how great ladies carry themselves on great occasions; he taught her how they relax. Uncle Pio and Calderón had trained her in beautiful Spanish; Don Andrés furnished her with the smart slang of *El Buen Retiro.*

Uncle Pio was made anxious by Camila's invitation from the Palace. He would have much preferred that she continue with her little vulgarian love-affairs in the theatrical ware-house. But when he saw that her art was gaining a new finish he was well content. He would sit in the back of the theatre, rolling about in his seat for sheer joy and amusement, watching the Perichole intimate to the audience that she frequented the great world about whom the dramatists wrote. She had a new way of fingering a wine-glass, of exchanging an adieu, a new way of entering a door that told everything. To Uncle Pio nothing else mattered. What was there in the world more lovely than a beautiful woman doing justice to a Spanish masterpiece?—a performance (he asks you), packed with observation, in which the very spacing of the words revealed a comment on life and on the text—delivered by a beautiful voice—illustrated by a faultless carriage, considerable personal beauty and irresistible charm. "We are almost ready to take this marvel to Spain," he would murmur to himself. After the performance he would go around to her dressing-room and say "Very good!" But before taking his leave he would manage to ask her where, in the name of the eleven thousand virgins of Cologne, she had acquired that affected way of saying *Excelencia.*

After a time the Viceroy asked the Perichole whether it would amuse her to invite a few discreet guests to their midnight suppers, and he asked her whether she would like to meet the Archbishop. Camila was delighted. The Archbishop was delighted. On the eve of their first meeting he sent the actress an emerald pendant as big as a playing-card.

There was something in Lima that was wrapped up in yards of violet satin from which protruded a great dropsical head and two fat pearly hands; and that was its archbishop. Between the rolls of flesh that surrounded them looked out two black eyes speaking discomfort, kindliness and wit. A curious and eager soul was imprisoned in all this lard, but by dint of never refusing himself a pheasant or a goose or his daily procession of Roman wines, he was his own bitter jailer. He loved his cathedral; he loved his duties; he was very devout. Some days he regarded his bulk ruefully; but the distress of remorse was less poignant than the distress of fasting and he was presently found deliberating over the secret messages that a certain roast sends to the certain salad that will follow it. And to punish himself he led an exemplary life in every other respect.

He had read all the literature of antiquity and forgotten all about it except a general aroma of charm and disillusion. He had been learned in the Fathers and the Councils and forgotten all about them save a floating impression of dissensions that had no application to Peru. He had read all the libertine masterpieces of Italy and France and reread them annually; even in the torments of the stone (happily dissolved by drinking the water from the springs of Santa María de Cluxambuqua), he could find nothing more nourishing than the anecdotes of Brantôme and the divine Aretino.

The Archbishop knew that most of the priests of Peru were scoundrels. It required all his delicate Epicurean education to prevent his doing something about it; he had to repeat over to himself his favourite notions: that the injustice and unhappiness in the world is a constant; that the theory of progress is a delusion; that the poor, never having known happiness, are insensible to misfortune. Like all the rich he could not bring himself to believe that the poor (look at their houses, look at their clothes) could really suffer. Like all the cultivated he believed that only the widely-read could be said to *know* that they were unhappy. On one occasion, the iniquities in his see having been called to his notice, he almost did something about it. He had just heard that it was becoming a rule in Peru for priests to exact two measures of meal for a fairly good absolution, and five measures, for a really effective one. He trembled with indignation; he roared to his secretary and bidding him bring up his writing materials, announced that he was going to dictate an overwhelming message to his shepherds. But there was no ink left in the inkwell; there was no ink left in the next room; there was no ink to be found in the whole palace. This state of things in his household so upset the good man that he fell ill of the combined rages and learned to guard himself against indignations.

The addition of the Archbishop to the suppers was so successful that Don Andrés began to think of new names.

He had grown increasingly dependent upon Uncle Pio, but waited until Camila should propose his inclusion of her own accord. And in due time Uncle Pio brought with him that courser of the seas, the Captain Alvarado. Generally the reunion had been several hours under way before Camila was able to join them after her performance at the theatre. She would arrive towards one o'clock, radiant and bejewelled and very tired. The four men received her as they would a great queen. For an hour or so she would carry the conversation, but gradually reclining more and more against Don Andrés' shoulder she would follow the talk as it flitted from one humorous lined face to the other. All night they talked, secretly comforting their hearts that longed always for Spain and telling themselves that such a symposium was after the manner of the high Spanish soul. They talked about ghosts and second-sight, and about the earth before man appeared upon it and about the possibility of the planets striking against one another; about whether the soul can be seen, like a dove, fluttering away at the moment of death; they wondered whether at the second coming of Christ to Jerusalem, Peru would be long in receiving the news. They talked until the sun rose, about wars and kings, about poets and scholars, and about strange countries. Each one poured into the conversation his store of wise sad anecdotes and his dry regret about the race of men. The flood of golden light struck across the Andes and entering the great window fell upon the piles of fruit, the stained brocade upon the table, and the sweet thoughtful forehead of the Perichole as she lay sleeping against the sleeve of her protector. There would ensue a long pause, no one wishing to make the first move to go, and the glances of them all would rest upon this strange beautiful bird who lived among them. But Uncle Pio's glance had been upon her all night, a quick glance from his black eyes, full of tenderness and anxiety, resting on the great secret and reason of his life.

But Uncle Pio never ceased watching Camila. He divided the inhabitants of this world into two groups, into those who had loved and those who had not. It was a horrible aristocracy, apparently, for those who had no capacity for love (or rather for suffering in love) could not be said to be alive and certainly would not live again after their death. They were a kind of straw population, filling the world with their meaningless laughter and tears and chatter and disappearing still lovable and vain into thin air. For this distinction he cultivated his own definition of love that was like no other and that had gathered all its bitterness and pride from his odd life. He regarded love as a sort of cruel malady through which the elect are required to pass in their late youth and from which they emerge, pale and wrung, but ready for the business of living. There was (he believed) a great repertory of errors mercifully impossible to human beings who had recovered from this illness. Unfortunately there remained to them a host of failings, but at least (from among many illustrations) they never mistook a protracted amiability for the whole conduct of life, they never again regarded any human being, from a prince to a servant, as a mechanical object. Uncle Pio never ceased watching Camila because it seemed to him that she had never undergone this initiation. In the months that followed her introduction to the Viceroy he held his breath and waited. He held his breath for years. Camila bore the Viceroy three children, yet remained the same. He knew that the first sign of her entrance into the true possession of the world would be the mastery of certain effects in her acting. There were certain passages in the plays that she would compass some day, simply, easily, and with secret joy, because they alluded to the new rich wisdom of her heart; but her treatment of such passages became more and more cursory, not to say embarrassed. He presently saw that she had tired of Don Andrés and had returned to a series of furtive love-affairs with the actors and matadors and merchants of the town.

She became more and more impatient of acting and another parasite found its way into her mind. She wanted to be a lady. She slowly contracted a greed for respectability and began to refer to her acting as a pastime. She acquired a duenna and some footmen and went to church at the fashionable hours. She attended the prize days at the University and appeared among the donors of the great charities. She even learned to read and write a little. Any faint discrimination against, her as a bohemian she challenged with fury. She led the Viceroy a horrible life with her passion for concessions and her gradual usurpation of privileges. The new vice displaced the old and she became noisily virtuous. She invented some parents and produced some cousins. She obtained an undocumented legitimatization of her children. In society she cultivated a delicate and languid magdelinism, as a great lady might, and she carried a candle in the penitential parades, side by side with ladies who had nothing to regret but an outburst of temper and a furtive glance into Descartes. Her sin had been acting and everyone knows that there were even saints who had been actors,—there was Saint Gelasius and Saint Genesius and Saint Margaret of Antioch and Saint Pelagia.

There was a fashionable watering place in the hills not far from Santa María de Cluxambuqua. Don Andrés had travelled in France and had thought to build himself a little mock Vichy; there was a pagoda, some drawing-rooms, a theatre, a little arena for bull-fights and some French gardens. Camila's health had never known a shadow, but she built herself a villa in the vicinity and sipped the hateful waters at eleven o'clock. The Marquesa de Montemayor has left a brilliant picture of this *opéra bouffe* paradise with the reigning divinity parading her fierce sensitiveness along the avenues of powdered shell and receiving the homage of all those who could not afford to offend the Viceroy. Doña María draws a portrait of this ruler, stately and weary, gambling all through the night in sums that would have raised another Escurial. And beside him she sets the portrait of his son, Camila's little Don Jaime. Don Jaime, at seven years, was a rachitic little body who seemed to have inherited not only his mother's forehead and eyes, but his father's liability to convulsions. He bore his pain with the silent bewilderment of an animal, and like an animal he was mortally ashamed when any evidences of it occurred in public. He was so beautiful that the more trivial forms of pity were hushed in his presence and his long thoughts about his difficulties had given his face a patient and startling dignity. His mother dressed him in garnet velvet, and when he was able he followed her about at a distance of several yards, extricating himself gravely from the ladies who tried to detain him in conversation. Camila was never cross to Don Jaime and she was never demonstrative. When the sun was shining the two could be seen walking along those artificial terraces in silence, Camila wondering when the felicity would begin that she had always associated with social position, Don Jaime rejoicing merely in the sunlight and anxiously estimating the approach of a cloud. They looked like figures that had strayed there from some remote country, or out of an old ballad, that had not yet learned the new language and had not yet found any friends.

Camila was about thirty when she left the stage and it required five years for her to achieve her place in society. She gradually became almost stout, though her head seemed to grow more beautiful every year. She took to overdressing and the floors of the drawing-rooms reflected a veritable tower of jewels and scarves and plumes. Her face and hands were covered with a bluish powder against which she drew an irritable mouth in scarlet and orange. The almost distraught fury of her temper was varied by the unnatural sweetness of her address in the company of the dowagers. In the earliest stages of her progress upward she had intimated to Uncle Pio that he was not to be seen with her in public, but finally she became impatient even of his discreeter visits. She conducted the interviews with formality and evasion. Her eyes never crossed his and she angled for pretexts to quarrel with him. Still he ventured out once a month to try her patience and when the call had become impossible he would climb the stairs and finish the hour among her children.

One day he arrived at her villa in the hills and, through her maid, begged for an opportunity to talk with her. He was told that she would see him in the French gardens a little before sunset. He had come up from Lima on a strange sentimental impulse. Like all solitary persons he had invested friendship with a divine glamour: he imagined that the people he passed on the street, laughing together and embracing when they parted, the people who dined together with so many smiles,—you will scarcely believe me, but he imagined that they were extracting from all that congeniality great store of satisfaction. So that suddenly he was filled with the excitement of seeing her again, of being called "Uncle Pio," and of reviving for a moment the trust and humour of their long vagabondage.

The French Gardens were at the southern end of the town. Behind them rose the higher Andes and before them there was a parapet overlooking a deep valley and overlooking wave after wave of hills that stretched toward the Pacific. It was the hour when bats fly low and the smaller animals play recklessly underfoot. A few solitaries lingered about the gardens, gazing dreamily into the sky that was being gradually emptied of its colour, or leaned upon the balustrade and looked down into the valley, noting in which village a dog was barking. It was the hour when the father returns home from the fields and plays for a moment in the yard with the dog that jumps upon him, holding his muzzle closed or throwing him upon his back. The young girls look about for the first star to fix a wish upon it, and the boys grow restless for supper. Even the busiest mother stands for a moment idle-handed, smiling at her dear and exasperating family.

Uncle Pio stood against one of the chipped marble benches and watched Camila coming towards him:

"I am late," she said. "I am sorry. What is it you wish to say to me?"

"Camila,—" he began.

"My name is Doña Micaela."

"I do not wish to offend you, Doña Micaela, but when you let me call you Camila for twenty years, I should think——"

"Oh, do as you like. Do as you like."

"Camila, promise me that you will listen to me. Promise me that you will not run away at my first sentence."

At once she burst out with unexpected passion: "Uncle Pio, listen to me. You are mad if you think you can make me return to the theatre. I look back at the theatre with horror. Understand that. The theatre! The theatre, indeed! The daily payment of insults in that filthy place. Understand that you are wasting your time."

He answered gently: "I would not have you come back if you are happy with these new friends."

"You don't like my new friends, then?" she answered quickly. "Whom do you offer me in their stead?"

"Camila, I only remember ..."

"I will not be criticized. I don't want any advice. It will be cold in a moment, I must go back to my house. Just give me up, that's all. Just put me out of your mind."

"Dear Camila, don't be angry. Let me talk to you. Just suffer me for ten minutes."

He did not understand why she was weeping. He did not know what to say. He talked at random: "You never even come to see the theatre, and they all notice it. The audiences are falling away now, too. They only put on the Old Comedy twice a week; all the other nights there are these new farces in prose. All is dull and childish and indecent. No one can speak Spanish any more. No one can even walk correctly any more. On Corpus Christi Day they gave *Belshazzar's Feast* where you were so wonderful. Now it was shameful."

There was a pause. A beautiful procession of clouds, like a flock of sheep, was straying up from the sea, slipping up the valleys between the hills. Camila suddenly touched his knee, and her face was like her face twenty years before: "Forgive me,

Uncle Pio, for being so bad. Jaime was ill this afternoon. There's nothing one can do. He lies there, so white and ... so surprised. One must just think of other things. Uncle Pio, it would be no good if I went back to the theatre. The audiences come for the prose farces. We were foolish to try and keep alive the Old Comedy. Let people read the old plays in books if they choose to. It is not worth while fighting with the crowd."

"Wonderful Camila, I was not just to you when you were on the stage. It was some foolish pride in me. I grudged you the praise that you deserved. Forgive me. You have always been a very great artist. If you come to see that you are not happy among these people you might think about going to Madrid. You would have a great triumph there. You are still young and beautiful. There will be time later to be called Doña Micaela. We shall be old soon. We shall be dead soon."

"No, I shall never see Spain. All the world is alike, Madrid or Lima."

"Oh, if we could go away to some island where the people would know you for yourself. And love you."

"You are fifty years old and you are still dreaming of such islands, Uncle Pio."

He bent his head and mumbled: "Of course I love you, Camila, as I always must and more than I can say. To have known you is enough for my whole life. You are a great lady now. And you are rich. There is no longer any way that I can help you. But I am always ready."

"How absurd you are," she said smiling. "You said that as boys say it. You don't seem to learn as you grow older, Uncle Pio. There is no such thing as that kind of love and that kind of island. It's in the theatre you find such things."

He look shamefaced, but unconvinced.

At last she rose and said sadly: "What are we talking about! It is growing cold. I must be going in. You must be resigned. I have no heart for the theatre." There was a pause. "And for the rest?... Oh, I do not understand. It is just circumstance. I must be what I must. Do not try to understand either. Don't think about me, Uncle Pio. Just forgive, that's all. Just try to forgive."

She stood still a moment, searching for something deeply felt to say to him. The first cloud reached the terrace; it was dark; the last stragglers were leaving the gardens. She was thinking of Don Jaime, and of Don Andrés and of himself. She could not find the words. Suddenly she bent down and kissed his fingers and went quickly away. But he sat for a long time in the gathering clouds trembling with happiness and trying to penetrate into the meaning of these things.

Suddenly the news was all over Lima. Doña Micaela Villegas, the lady that used to be Camila the Perichole, had the small-pox. Several hundred other persons had the small-pox also, but popular interest and malignity were concentrated upon the actress. A wild hope ran about the town that the beauty would be impaired that had enabled her to despise the class from which she sprang. The news escaped from the sick-room that Camila had become ludicrous in homeliness and the cup of the envious overflowed. As soon as she was able she had herself carried from the city to her villa in the hills; she ordered the sale of her elegant little palace. She returned her jewels to their givers and she sold her fine clothes. The Viceroy, the Archbishop, and the few men at court who had been her sincerest admirers besieged her door still with messages and gifts; the messages were ignored and the gifts were returned without comment. No one but her nurse and maids had been permitted to see her since the commencement of her illness. As an answer to his repeated attempts Don Andrés received a large sum of money from her with a letter compounded of all that is possible in bitterness and pride.

Like all beautiful women who have been brought up amid continual tributes to her beauty she assumed without cynicism that it must necessarily be the basis of anyone's attachment to herself; henceforth any attention paid to her must spring from a pity full of condescension and faintly perfumed with satisfaction at so complete a reversal. This assumption that she need look for no more devotion now that her beauty had passed proceeded from the fact that she had never realized any love save love as passion. Such love, though it expends itself in generosity and thoughtfulness, though it give birth to visions and to great poetry, remains among the sharpest expressions of self-interest. Not until it has passed through a long servitude, through its own self-hatred, through

mockery, through great doubts, can it take its place among the loyalties. Many who have spent a lifetime in it can tell us less of love than the child that lost a dog yesterday. As her friends continued in their efforts to draw her again into society she grew more and more angry and dispatched insulting messages to the city. It was said for a time that she was retiring into religion. But new rumours that all was fury and despair on the little farm, contradicted the old. For those near to her the despair was fearful to behold. She was convinced that her life was over, her life and children's. In her hysterical pride she had given back more than she owed and the approach of poverty was added to the loneliness and the gloom of her future. There was nothing left for her to do but to draw out her days in jealous solitude in the center of the little farm that was falling into decay. She brooded for hours upon the joy of her enemies and could be heard striding about her room with strange cries.

Uncle Pio did not allow himself to be discouraged. By dint of making himself useful to the children, by taking a hand in the management of the farm and by discreetly lending her some money he obtained his entrance into the house and even into the presence of its veiled mistress. But even then Camila, convinced in her pride that he *pitied* her, lashed him with the blade of her tongue and derived some strange comfort from heaping him with sneers. He loved her the more, understanding better than she did herself all the stages in the convalescence of her humiliated spirit. But one day an accident befell that lost him his share in her progress. He pushed open a door.

She thought she had locked it. For just one hour a foolish secret hope had come to her; she wondered whether she could make a paste of chalk and cream to spread upon her face. She who had sneered so often at the befloured grandmothers of the court wondered for a few moments whether she had learned anything on the stage that would aid her now. She thought she had locked the door and with hurried hands and beating heart she laid on the coat, the grotesque pallor, and as she gazed into the mirror and recognized the futility of her attempt she caught the image of Uncle Pio standing in the door amazed. She rose from the chair with a cry and covered her face with her hands.

"Go away. Go away out of my house forever," she screamed. "I never want to see you again." In her shame she drove him out with blasphemy and hatred, she pursued him down the corridor and hurled objects down the stairs. She gave her farmer orders that Uncle Pio was forbidden to come into the grounds. But he continued for a week trying to see her again. At last he went back to Lima; he filled in the time as best he could, but he longed to be by her as a boy of eighteen would long. At last he devised a stratagem and returned up into the hills to put it into effect.

One morning before dawn he arose and lay on the ground below her window. He imitated in the darkness the sound of weeping, and, as nearly as he could, of a young girl's weeping. He

continued in this for the whole quarter of an hour. He did not let his voice rise above that degree of loudness which Italian musicians would represent by the direction piano, but he frequently intermitted the sound trusting that if she were asleep it would insinuate itself into her mind as well by duration as by degree. The air was cool and agreeable. The first faint streak of sapphire was appearing behind the peaks and in the east the star of morning was pulsating every moment with a more tender intention. A profound silence wrapped all the farm buildings, only an occasional breeze set all the grasses sighing. Suddenly a lamp was lit in her room and a moment later the shutter was thrown back and a head wrapped in veils leaned far out.

"Who is there?" asked the beautiful voice.

Uncle Pio remained silent.

Camila said again in a tone edged with impatience:

"Who is there? Who is there weeping?"

"Doña Micaela, my lady, I beg of you to come here to me."

"Who are you and what do you want?"

"I am a poor girl. I am Estrella. I beg of you to come and help me. Do not call your maid. I pray you, Doña Micaela, to come yourself."

Camila was silent a moment, then said abruptly: "Very well," and closed the shutter. Presently she appeared around the corner of the house. She wore a thick cloak that dragged in the dew. She stood at a distance and said: "Come over here to where I am standing,—Who are you?"

Uncle Pio rose up. "Camila, it is I,—Uncle Pio. Forgive me, but I must speak to you."

"Mother of God, when shall I be free of this dreadful person! Understand: I want to see no one. I don't want to speak to a soul. My life is over. That is all."

"Camila, by our long life together, I beg of you to grant me one thing. I shall go away and never trouble you again."

"I grant you nothing, nothing. Stay away from me."

"I promise you I shall never trouble you again if you listen to me this once." She was hurrying around to the door on the other side of the house and Uncle Pio was obliged to run beside her to make sure that she heard what he was saying. She stopped:

"What is it then? Hurry. It is cold. I am not well. I must go back to my room."

"Camila, let me take Don Jaime for a year to live with me in Lima. Let me be his teacher. Let me teach him the Castilian. Here he is left among the servants. He is learning nothing."

"No."

"Camila, what will become of him? He has a good mind and he wants to learn."

"He is sick. He is delicate. Your house is a sty. Only the country is good for him."

"But he has been much better these last few months. I promise you I shall clean out my house. I shall apply to Madre María del Pilar for a housekeeper. Here he is in your stables all day. I shall teach him all that a gentleman should know,—fencing and Latin and music. We shall read all...."

"A mother cannot be separated from her child like that. It is impossible. You are crazy to have thought of it. Give up thinking of me and of everything about me. I no longer exist. I and my children will get on as best we can. Do not try to disturb me again. I do not want to see any human being."

Now it was that Uncle Pio felt obliged to use a hard measure. "Then pay me the money that you owe me," he said.

Camila stood still, confounded. To herself she said: "Life is too fearful to bear. When may I die?" After a moment she answered him, in a hoarse voice: "I have very little money. I will pay you what I can. I will pay you now. I have a few jewels here. Then we need never see one another again." She was ashamed of her poverty. She took a few steps, then turned and said: "Now I see that you are a very hard man. But it is right that I pay you what I owe you."

"No, Camila, I only said that to enforce my request. I shall take no money from you. But lend me Don Jaime for one year. I shall love him and take every care of him. Did I harm you? Was I a bad teacher to you in those other years?"

"It is cruel of you to keep urging gratitude, gratitude, gratitude. I was grateful,—good, good! but now that I am no longer the same woman there remains nothing to be grateful for." There was a silence. Her eyes were resting on the star that seemed to be leading forth the whole sky in its wonder. A great pain lay at her heart, the pain of a world that was meaningless. Then she said: "If Jaime wishes to go with you, very well. I shall talk to, him in the morning. If he wishes to go with you, you will find him at the Inn about noon. Good night. Go with God."

"Go with God."

★ ★ ★

SHE RETURNED TO THE HOUSE. The next day the grave little boy appeared at the Inn. His fine clothes were torn and stained now and he carried a small bundle for change. His mother had given him a gold piece for spending-money and a little stone that shown in the dark to look at in his sleepless nights. They set off together in a cart, but soon Uncle Pio became aware that the jolting was not good for the boy. He carried him on his shoulder. As they drew near to the bridge of San Luis Rey, Jaime tried to conceal his shame for he knew that one of those moments was coming that separated him from other people. He was especially ashamed because Uncle Pio had just overtaken a friend of his, a sea-captain. And just as they got to the bridge he spoke to an old lady who was travelling with a little girl. Uncle Pio said that when they had crossed the bridge they would sit down and rest, but it turned out not to be necessary.

TO BE CONCLUDED IN LITERARY OUTLAW #4

QUEEN OF THE SAGEBRUSH FRONTIER
FIREHAIR
by JOHN STARR
IT HAPPENED YESTERDAY— YESTERDAY, WHEN AMERICA WAS WILD AND RAW AND YOUNG... BEGINNING AN EPIC STORY OF THE WEST THAT WILL NEVER DIE. AND OF A GIRL THAT FATE NAMED "FIREHAIR."

THROUGH THE SOLITARY SUN-PARCHED STREET OF PLAINSVILLE, AN EVER SHIFTING TIDE OF ADVENTURERS CONSTANTLY FLOWED ON TOWARD THE DISTANT ROLLING PRAIRIES AND SNOW TOPPED MOUNTAINS OF THE UNSETTLED WEST. A DETERMINED RACE OF MEN, SEEKING TO MAKE SOME LONG CHERISHED DREAM COME TRUE... BUT SOME FEW CHOSE TO LINGER WITHIN THOSE HEAT-WARPED WALLS... AND WATCH...
THERE SHE COMES, FINGERS-THE JUNCTION STAGE! WHAT'S ABOARD THAT'S GOT YOU SO ITCHY?
SIX THOUSAND EASY DOLLARS- I HOPE!
AAH- AN' THERE IT IS. THEM CRATES ON TOP!
LAST STOP, FOLKS- ALL OUT!
HERE WE ARE, PRINCESS - THE JUMP-OFF PLACE ...OUR GATEWAY TO A BRAVE NEW LIFE!
OH, DAD- I'M SO EXCITED!
FROM NOW ON, WE'RE WESTERNERS, PRINCESS... BOSTON, THE PAST- WE'LL FORGET IT ALL, EH?
IF YOU SAY SO, DAD.
HEY - STRANGER!
YO'RE J.B. SMITH, I RECKON... I'M CATAMOUNT KELLY, TRAIL BOSS, AN' I GOT YUH BOOKED WITH MY TRAIN PULLIN' OUT AT NOON.
FINE, MR. KELLY- WE'LL BE READY.

SOON...
HURRY, PRINCESS— OUR WAGON'S WAITING!
BUT I-I-LOOK SO QUEER, DAD!

A NEW COUNTRY, NEW CLOTHES, A NEW NAME—I FEEL LIKE A STRANGER TO MYSELF!
HMM...LOADIN' TH' RIFLE CRATES IN WAGON NUMBER FIVE, EH?

YORE DUFFEL'S IN WAGON THREE, MR. SMITH...HOP ABOARD AN' LE'S RAMBLE!
COME ON, PRINCESS— WE'RE OFF!

THIS IS YOUR PUMPKIN COACH, MY DEAR—BOUND FOR ADVENTURE... GET ALONG—YOU MULES!
HURRY, MULES— AND FIND ME MY PRINCE CHARMING!

THERE THEY GO...TEN MORE WAGONLOADS OF FOOLS HEADED FOR HELL'S BONEYARDS!
YOU MEAN REDSKINS, FINGERS?

I MEAN THAT SMART MEN HUNT THEIR FORTUNES CLOSER TO HOME...S'LONG KID. I'LL SEE YUH WHEN I SEE YUH!
3

ABOARD THE WAGON-TRAIN.
THERE'S ONE THING I HAVEN'T MENTIONED, PRINCESS—
THIS KEY OPENS THE BLACK BOX IN MY LUGGAGE... THE DEVILS WE'RE RUNNING AWAY FROM ARE LOCKED TIGHT INSIDE...
NEXT MORNING
BUT DON'T OPEN THE BOX, MY DEAR, UNLESS SOMETHING HAPPENS TO ME!
I WON'T, DAD!
HOW SOON BEFORE WE HIT THE INJUN COUNTRY, RED?
DON'T WORRY, PILGRIM— LEAVE THAT TO US SCOUTS.
THE U.S. CAVALRY HAS GOT THE PLAINS REDSKINS PLUMB TAMED, WE WON'T SIGHT HOSS-TILE SMOKE UNTIL WE CUT TH' COLORADO!
STOW THE PALAVER AN' CLIMB IN YORE SADDLES! WE'RE ON TH' MOVE!
OKAY, CAT!
...BUT AS THE WAGONS CRAWL ALONG, EVIL EYES KEEP A BUZZARD'S VIGIL... AND AS THE THIRD DAY'S SUNSET NEARS —
4

WHERE BOSS? TELLUM WAGON-SNAKE SOON DRINK WHERE RIVER MAD!
HERE'S YOUR SPY, FINGERS! SAYS KELLY'S TRAIN WILL REACH SAW-TOOTH FORD BY SUNDOWN.
GOOD!

EXACTLY AS I FIGGERED IT. WE'LL LAY OUR AMBUSH ON THAT BRUSH SLOPE NORTH—

AN' OUR CHARGE WILL PIN 'EM BETWEEN HOT LEAD AN' THE RAPIDS...LET'S GO!

BUT DON'T KILL 'EM ALL, BOYS! LEAVE A FEW TO TELL IT WAS INJUNS WHO RAIDED 'EM!

LATER...WITH SUNSET NEAR—
HERE'S WHERE WE FORD ACROSS, SMITH...KEEP A GOOD REIN ON YORE TEAM!
SURE WILL, CAT!

NOT A SINGLE DELAY OR ACCIDENT SINCE WE STARTED! THAT'S ALMOST A RECORD, ISN'T IT?
RECORD—IT'S DANG NIGH A MIRACLE!

BUT ABOVE—
IT'S CAT KELLY ON THAT HOSS! CAN YUH WING 'IM, CROWFOOT?
HUH! HEAP EASY—

SOME OF THE YOUNG BUCKS—BEGGIN' YORE PARDON, MISS—SAY THAT YO'RE OUR GOOD LUCK—

DADDY—DADDY!
JUMPIN' JEHOSOPHAT—INJUNS!!

HE FELL ON THE WHEELERS—THEY'RE BOLTING!

DAD—DAD! I CAN'T HOLD THEM! HELP—HELP!

6

THEN DEVIL-YELLS AND GUNBLAST...
YA-WEE—YA-HEEE!
YIIII—EEE!
...AND THE RENEGADES OF DEATH ATTACKING—

SHOOT TH' HOSSES! HERD 'EM INTO TH' RIVER!
HAII— EEE!

GUNS EXPLODING—TERROR SCREAMING! MURDER ON THE PROD—
AND PANIC SWEEPS THE AMBUSHED WAGON-TRAIN...

DON'T LET 'EM MILL YUH, BOYS! LAY LOW AN' PICK 'EM OFF!
BETTER TAKE COVER YORE-SELF, CAT!

THEY'RE PAINTED UP LIKE YALLER-KNIVES, BUT THEY YELL LIKE 'RAPAHOES—

CAT'S DOWN! THEY GOT 'IM!
THEY'RE CLOSIN' IN! MAKE EVERY BULLET COUNT!
7.

BUT THE RENEGADE GUNS WERE THREE TO ONE...AND THE REST WAS MASSACRE!

THAT'S THE CLEANUP, FINGERS... MEBBEE SIX GOT OFF ALIVE.
GOOD... LET'S TAKE A LOOK AT THAT RUNAWAY WAGON THOUGH!
HMM... SEARCH THE BAGGAGE CLOSE, BLACKIE! PLENTY OF THESE PILGRIMS FLASHED BIG ROLLS OF YALLERBACKS IN TOWN!
DEAD... NOT A TRINKET ON HER... PRETTY LITTLE DEVIL, THOUGH!
NO LUCK, BLACKIE?
JUST THIS LOCKED SATCHEL... I'LL STOW IT WITH THE OTHER STUFF!
JUST ABOUT LOADED, FINGERS—WHATTA' HAUL!
WE'LL FIRE THE OTHER WAGONS' AN' VAMOOSE... SHAKE A LEG, BOYS!
...BUT AS THE RAIDERS RIDE THEIR LOOT TOWARD THE CRIMSONED HILLS, A HIDDEN WATCHER COMES ALIVE...

THEY WORE THE WAR-PAINT OF OUR TRIBE, YET THEY SPOKE IN PALEFACE VOICES... HOLD ON! WHAT SOUND IS THAT?
DEATH IN HER FACE YET HER HEART STILL BEATS... WHAT MUST I DO?
STEADY, SNAKE-EYE! WE TAKE HER TO OUR TENTS SO THAT SHE MAY LIVE TO SPEAK THE TRUTH.
AND THUS — THE-GIRL-WITHOUT-A-NAME CAME TO THE HUNTING CAMP OF TEHAMA'S TRIBE ON CROOKED RIVER...
HO! THERE IS NEED OF TWO HORNS AND HIS MEDICINES!
TELL YOUR FATHER LITTLE AX, THAT HIS SON IS A FOOL... A WISE MAN WOULD HAVE LEFT HER... BUT I WILL DO WHAT MAY BE DONE FOR HER!

NEXT MORNING, IN THE MEDICINE TENT...
SHE STIRS! SHE RETURNS FROM THE VALLEY OF SHADOWS!

D-DAD...HE'S FALLING! THE MULES—I CAN'T STOP THEM!

SHE WILL LIVE, LITTLE AX, BUT HER MIND IS STILL LOST IN TERROR.
THE COUNCIL MEETS NOW... BRING HER TO THEM.

...AND THE JUDGMENT DRUMS THROB SOLEMNLY AS THE ELDERS ENTER THE TENT OF CHIEF TEHAMA...

WE WILL BE SADDLED WITH THE CRIMES OF THE PALEFACE KILLERS!
AYEE! WE MUST BREAK CAMP AND FLEE TO THE HILLS!
THE WHITE MAID IS PROOF AGAINST US—GET RID OF HER!

HOLD! I, TEHAMA, YOUR CHIEF BY THE SACRED SIGN, TAKE UPON MYSELF ALL EVIL MY OWN SON BRINGS... LET HIM SPEAK!

THIS MAIDEN OF THE FIREHAIR IS THE LIVING PROOF WE NEED AGAINST THE WHITE MAN'S MURDER LIES... IS THAT WHAT YOU WOULD SAY, MY SON?
YES, MY FATHER... THE BLACK OF DEATH STILL SHADES HER MIND- SHE CANNOT SPEAK HER NAME- BUT UNTIL SHE CAN -
I CLAIM HER MY CAPTIVE BY THE ANCIENT LAWS- AND MY KNIFE DEFENDS THE CLAIM!
IT IS CRAZY, O, TEHAMA! WHAT WARRIOR WOULD FIGHT A HALF-GROWN BOY?
YET- THE LAW IS THE LAW...AND THE KNIFE OF LITTLE AX HAS SPOKEN IT!
MY HEAD...WHERE AM I? WHO AM I? WHY- WHY CAN'T I THINK?
SHE IS MINE, GREAT SPIRIT- MY SISTER...AND I WILL MAKE HER WELL AND CARE FOR HER!
...AND SO IT WAS THAT SHE CAME TO THE TEPEES OF TEHAMA'S TRIBE ...THE GIRL WHO COULD REMEMBER ONLY THAT SHE ONCE HAD LIVED IN ANOTHER WORLD AND THAT A VOICE SHE LOVED HAD CALLED HER "PRINCESS"...AND THE DAYS PASSED AND THE SEASONS CHANGED, AND TOMORROW SHE WOULD WIN THE NAME THAT THE WESTERN WINDS HAVE CARRIED FAR—
FIREHAIR!

THE ADVENTURES OF PENROD

BY BOOTH TARKINGTON

CHAPTER VII
EVILS OF DRINK

NEXT DAY, PENROD ACQUIRED A DIME by a simple and antique process which was without doubt sometimes practised by the boys of Babylon. When the teacher of his class in Sunday-school requested the weekly contribution, Penrod, fumbling honestly (at first) in the wrong pockets, managed to look so embarrassed that the gentle lady told him not to mind, and said she was often forgetful herself. She was so sweet about it that, looking into the future, Penrod began to feel confident of a small but regular income.

At the close of the afternoon services he did not go home, but proceeded to squander the funds just withheld from China upon an orgy of the most pungently forbidden description. In a Drug Emporium, near the church, he purchased a five-cent sack of candy consisting for the most part of the heavily flavoured hoofs of horned cattle, but undeniably substantial, and so generously capable of resisting solution that the purchaser must needs be avaricious beyond reason who did not realize his money's worth.

Equipped with this collation, Penrod contributed his remaining nickel to a picture show, countenanced upon the seventh day by the legal but not the moral authorities. Here, in cozy darkness, he placidly insulted his liver with jaw-breaker upon jaw-breaker from the paper sack, and in a surfeit of content watched the silent actors on the screen.

One film made a lasting impression upon him. It depicted with relentless pathos the drunkard's progress; beginning with his conversion to beer in the company of loose travelling men; pursuing him through an inexplicable lapse into evening clothes and the society of some remarkably painful ladies, next, exhibiting the effects of alcohol on the victim's domestic disposition, the unfortunate man was seen in the act of striking his wife and, subsequently, his pleading baby daughter with an abnormally heavy walking-stick. Their flight—through the snow—to seek the protection of a relative was shown, and finally, the drunkard's picturesque behaviour at the portals of a madhouse.

So fascinated was Penrod that he postponed his departure until this film came round again, by which time he had finished his unnatural repast and almost, but not quite, decided against following the profession of a drunkard when he grew up.

Emerging, satiated, from the theatre, a public timepiece before a jeweller's shop confronted him with an unexpected dial and imminent perplexities. How was he to explain at home these hours of dalliance? There was a steadfast rule that he return direct from Sunday-school; and Sunday rules were important, because on that day there was his father, always at home and at hand, perilously ready for action. One of the hardest conditions of boyhood is the almost continuous strain put upon the powers of invention by the constant and harassing necessity for explanations of every natural act.

Proceeding homeward through the deepening twilight as rapidly as possible, at a gait half skip and half canter, Penrod made up his mind in what manner he would account for his long delay, and, as he drew nearer, rehearsed in words the opening passage of his defence.

"Now see here," he determined to begin; "I do not wished to be blamed for things I couldn't help, nor any other boy. I was going along the street by a cottage and a lady put her head out of the window and said her husband was drunk and whipping her and her little girl, and she asked me wouldn't I come in and help hold him. So I went in and tried to get hold of this drunken lady's husband where he was whipping their baby daughter, but he wouldn't pay any attention, and I TOLD her I ought to be getting home, but she kep' on askin' me to stay——"

At this point he reached the corner of his own yard, where a coincidence not only checked the rehearsal of his eloquence but happily obviated all occasion for it. A cab from the station drew up in front of the gate, and there descended a troubled lady in black and a fragile little girl about three. Mrs. Schofield rushed from the house and enfolded both in hospitable arms.

They were Penrod's Aunt Clara and cousin, also Clara, from Dayton, Illinois, and in the flurry of their arrival everybody forgot to put Penrod to the question. It is doubtful, however, if he felt any relief; there may have been even a slight, unconscious disappointment not altogether dissimilar to that of an actor deprived of a good part.

In the course of some really necessary preparations for dinner he stepped from the bathroom into the pink-and-white bedchamber of his sister, and addressed her rather thickly through a towel.

"When'd mamma find out Aunt Clara and Cousin Clara were coming?"

"Not till she saw them from the window. She just happened to look out as they drove up. Aunt Clara telegraphed this morning, but it wasn't delivered."

"How long they goin' to stay?"

"I don't know."

Penrod ceased to rub his shining face, and thoughtfully tossed the towel through the bathroom door. "Uncle John won't try to make 'em come back home, I guess, will he?" (Uncle John was Aunt Clara's husband, a successful manufacturer of stoves, and his lifelong regret was that he had not entered the Baptist ministry.) "He'll let 'em stay here quietly, won't he?"

"What ARE you talking about?" demanded Margaret, turning from her mirror. "Uncle John sent them here. Why shouldn't he let them stay?"

Penrod looked crestfallen. "Then he hasn't taken to drink?"

"Certainly not!" She emphasized the denial with a pretty peal of soprano laughter.

"Then why," asked her brother gloomily, "why did Aunt Clara look so worried when she got here?"

"Good gracious! Don't people worry about anything except somebody's drinking? Where did you get such an idea?"

"Well," he persisted, "you don't KNOW it ain't that."

She laughed again, wholeheartedly. "Poor Uncle John! He won't even allow grape juice or ginger ale in his house. They came because they were afraid little Clara might catch the measles. She's very delicate, and there's such an epidemic of measles among the children over in Dayton the schools had to be closed. Uncle John got so worried that last night he dreamed about it; and this morning he couldn't stand it any longer and packed them off over here, though he thinks its wicked to travel on Sunday. And Aunt Clara was worried when she got here because they'd forgotten to check her trunk and it will have to

be sent by express. Now what in the name of the common sense put it into your head that Uncle John had taken to———"

"Oh, nothing." He turned lifelessly away and went downstairs, a new-born hope dying in his bosom. Life seems so needlessly dull sometimes.

CHAPTER VIII
SCHOOL

NEXT MORNING, WHEN HE HAD ONCE more resumed the dreadful burden of education, it seemed infinitely duller. And yet what pleasanter sight is there than a schoolroom well filled with children of those sprouting years just before the 'teens? The casual visitor, gazing from the teacher's platform upon these busy little heads, needs only a blunted memory to experience the most agreeable and exhilarating sensations. Still, for the greater part, the children are unconscious of the happiness of their condition; for nothing is more pathetically true than that we "never know when we are well off." The boys in a public school are less aware of their happy state than are the girls; and of all the boys in his room, probably Penrod himself had the least appreciation of his felicity.

He sat staring at an open page of a textbook, but not studying; not even reading; not even thinking. Nor was he lost in a reverie: his mind's eye was shut, as his physical eye might well have been, for the optic nerve, flaccid with ennui, conveyed nothing whatever of the printed page upon which the orb of vision was partially focused. Penrod was doing something very unusual and rare, something almost never accomplished except by coloured people or by a boy in school on a spring day: he was doing really nothing at all. He was merely a state of being.

From the street a sound stole in through the open window, and abhorring Nature began to fill the vacuum called Penrod Schofield; for the sound was the spring song of a mouth-organ, coming down the sidewalk. The windows were intentionally above the level of the eyes of the seated pupils; but the picture of the musician was plain to Penrod, painted for him by a quality in the runs and trills, partaking of the oboe, of the calliope, and of cats in anguish; an excruciating sweetness obtained only by the wallowing, walloping yellow-pink palm of a hand whose back was Congo black and shiny. The music came down the street and passed beneath the window, accompanied by the care-free shuffling of a pair of old shoes scuffing syncopations on the cement sidewalk. It passed into the distance; became faint and blurred; was gone. Emotion stirred in Penrod a great and poignant desire, but (perhaps fortunately) no fairy godmother made her appearance.

Otherwise Penrod would have gone down the street in a black skin, playing the mouth-organ, and an unprepared coloured youth would have found himself enjoying educational advantages for which he had no ambition whatever.

Roused from perfect apathy, the boy cast about the schoolroom an eye wearied to nausea by the perpetual vision of the neat teacher upon the platform, the backs of the heads of the pupils in front of him, and the monotonous stretches of blackboard threateningly defaced by arithmetical formulae and other insignia of torture. Above the blackboard, the walls of the high room were of white plaster—white with the qualified whiteness of old snow in a soft coal town. This dismal expanse was broken by four lithographic portraits, votive offerings of a thoughtful publisher. The portraits were of good and great men, kind men; men who loved children. Their faces were noble and benevolent. But the lithographs offered the only rest for the eyes of children fatigued by the everlasting sameness of the schoolroom. Long day after long day, interminable week in and interminable week out, vast month on vast month, the pupils sat with those four portraits beaming kindness down upon them. The faces became permanent in the consciousness of the children; they became an obsession—in and out of school the children were never free of them. The four faces haunted the minds of children falling asleep; they hung upon the minds of children waking at night; they rose forebodingly in the minds of children waking in the morning; they became monstrously alive in the minds of children lying sick of fever. Never, while the children of that schoolroom lived, would they be able to forget one detail of the four lithographs: the hand of Longfellow was fixed, for them, forever, in his beard. And by a simple and unconscious association of ideas, Penrod Schofield was accumulating an antipathy for the gentle Longfellow and for James Russell Lowell and for Oliver Wendell Holmes and for John Greenleaf Whittier, which would never permit him to peruse a work of one of those great New Englanders without a feeling of personal resentment.

His eyes fell slowly and inimically from the brow of Whittier to the braid of reddish hair belonging to Victorine Riordan, the little octoroon girl who sat directly in front of him. Victorine's back was as familiar to Penrod as the necktie of Oliver Wendell Holmes. So was her gayly coloured plaid waist. He hated the waist as he hated Victorine herself, without knowing why. Enforced companionship in large quantities and on an equal basis between the sexes appears to sterilize the affections, and schoolroom romances are few.

Victorine's hair was thick, and the brickish glints in it were beautiful, but Penrod was very tired of it. A tiny knot of green ribbon finished off the braid and kept it from unravelling; and beneath the ribbon there was a final wisp of hair which was just long enough to repose upon Penrod's desk when Victorine leaned back in her seat. It was there now. Thoughtfully, he took the braid between thumb and forefinger, and, without disturbing Victorine, dipped the end of it and the green ribbon into the inkwell of his desk. He brought hair and ribbon forth dripping purple ink, and partially dried them on a blotter, though,

a moment later when Victorine leaned forward, they were still able to add a few picturesque touches to the plaid waist.

Rudolph Krauss, across the aisle from Penrod, watched the operation with protuberant eyes, fascinated. Inspired to imitation, he took a piece of chalk from his pocket and wrote "RATS" across the shoulder-blades of the boy in front of him, then looked across appealingly to Penrod for tokens of congratulation. Penrod yawned. It may not be denied that at times he appeared to be a very self-centred boy.

CHAPTER IX
SOARING

HALF THE MEMBERS OF THE CLASS passed out to a recitation-room, the empurpled Victorine among them, and Miss Spence started the remaining half through the ordeal of trial by mathematics. Several boys and girls were sent to the blackboard, and Penrod, spared for the moment, followed their operations a little while with his eyes, but not with his mind; then, sinking deeper in his seat, limply abandoned the effort. His eyes remained open, but saw nothing; the routine of the arithmetic lesson reached his ears in familiar, meaningless sounds, but he heard nothing; and yet, this time, he was profoundly occupied. He had drifted away from the painful land of facts, and floated now in a new sea of fancy which he had just discovered.

Maturity forgets the marvellous realness of a boy's day-dreams, how colourful they glow, rosy and living, and how opaque the curtain closing down between the dreamer and the actual world. That curtain is almost sound-proof, too, and causes more throat-trouble among parents than is suspected.

The nervous monotony of the schoolroom inspires a sometimes unbearable longing for something astonishing to happen, and as every boy's fundamental desire is to do something astonishing himself, so as to be the centre of all human interest and awe, it was natural that Penrod should discover in fancy the delightful secret of self-levitation. He found, in this curious series of imaginings, during the lesson in arithmetic, that the atmosphere may be navigated as by a swimmer under water, but with infinitely greater ease and with perfect comfort in breathing. In his mind he extended his arms gracefully, at a level with his shoulders, and delicately paddled the air with his hands, which at once caused him to be drawn up out of his seat and elevated gently to a position about midway between the floor and the ceiling, where he came to an equilibrium and floated; a sensation not the less exquisite because of the screams of his fellow pupils, appalled by the miracle. Miss Spence herself was amazed and frightened, but he only smiled down carelessly upon her when she commanded him to return to earth; and then, when she climbed upon a desk to pull him down, he quietly paddled himself a little higher, leaving his toes just out of her reach. Next, he swam through a few slow somersaults to show his mastery of the new art, and, with the shouting of the dumfounded scholars ringing in his ears, turned on his side and floated swiftly out of the window, immediately rising above the housetops, while people in the street below him shrieked, and a trolley car stopped dead in wonder.

With almost no exertion he paddled himself, many yards at a stroke, to the girls' private school where Marjorie Jones was a pupil—Marjorie Jones of the amber curls and the golden voice! Long before the "Pageant of the Table Round," she had offered Penrod a hundred proofs that she considered him wholly undesirable and ineligible. At the Friday Afternoon Dancing Class she consistently incited and led the laughter at him whenever Professor Bartet singled him out for admonition in matters of feet and decorum. And but yesterday she had chid him for his slavish lack of memory in daring to offer her a greeting on the way to Sunday-school. "Well! I expect you must forgot I told you never to speak to me again! If I was a boy, I'd be too proud to come hanging around people that don't speak to me, even if I WAS the Worst Boy in Town!" So she flouted him. But now, as he floated in through the window of her classroom and swam gently along the ceiling like an escaped toy balloon, she fell upon her knees beside her little desk, and, lifting up her arms toward him, cried with love and admiration:

"Oh, PENrod!"

He negligently kicked a globe from the high chandelier, and, smiling coldly, floated out through the hall to the front steps of the school, while Marjorie followed, imploring him to grant her one kind look.

In the street an enormous crowd had gathered, headed by Miss Spence and a brass band; and a cheer from a hundred thousand throats shook the very ground as Penrod swam overhead. Marjorie knelt upon the steps and watched adoringly while Penrod took the drum-major's baton and, performing sinuous evolutions above the crowd, led the band. Then he threw the baton so high that it disappeared from sight; but he went swiftly after it, a double delight, for he had not only the delicious sensation of rocketing safely up and up into the blue sky, but also that of standing in the crowd below, watching and admiring himself as he dwindled to a speck, disappeared and then, emerging from a cloud, came speeding down, with the baton in his hand, to the level of the treetops, where he beat time for the band and the vast throng and Marjorie Jones, who all united in the "Star-spangled Banner" in honour of his aerial achievements. It was a great moment.

It was a great moment, but something seemed to threaten it. The face of Miss Spence looking up from the crowd grew too vivid—unpleasantly vivid. She was beckoning him and shouting, "Come down, Penrod Schofield! Penrod Schofield, come down here!"

He could hear her above the band and the singing of the multitude; she seemed intent on spoiling everything. Marjorie Jones was weeping to show how sorry she was that she had formerly slighted him, and throwing kisses to prove that she loved him; but Miss Spence kept jumping between him and Marjorie, incessantly calling his name.

He grew more and more irritated with her; he was the most important person in the world and was engaged in proving it to Marjorie Jones and the whole city, and yet Miss Spence seemed to feel she still had the right to order him about as she did in the old days when he was an ordinary schoolboy. He was furious; he was sure she wanted him to do something disagreeable. It seemed to him that she had screamed "Penrod Schofield!" thousands of times.

From the beginning of his aerial experiments in his own schoolroom, he had not opened his lips, knowing somehow that one of the requirements for air floating is perfect silence on the part of the floater; but, finally, irritated beyond measure by Miss Spence's clamorous insistence, he was unable to restrain an indignant rebuke and immediately came to earth with a frightful bump.

Miss Spence—in the flesh—had directed toward the physical body of the absent Penrod an inquiry as to the fractional consequences of dividing seventeen apples, fairly, among three boys, and she was surprised and displeased to receive no answer although to the best of her knowledge and belief, he was looking fixedly at her. She repeated her question crisply, without visible effect; then summoned him by name with increasing asperity. Twice she called him, while all his fellow pupils turned to stare at the gazing boy. She advanced a step from the platform.

"Penrod Schofield!"

"Oh, my goodness!" he shouted suddenly. "Can't you keep still a MINUTE?"

CHAPTER X
UNCLE JOHN

Miss Spence gasped. So did the pupils.

The whole room filled with a swelling conglomerate "O-O-O-O-H!"

As for Penrod himself, the walls reeled with the shock. He sat with his mouth open, a mere lump of stupefaction. For the appalling words that he had hurled at the teacher were as inexplicable to him as to any other who heard them.

Nothing is more treacherous than the human mind; nothing else so loves to play the Iscariot. Even when patiently bullied into a semblance of order and training, it may prove but a base and shifty servant. And Penrod's mind was not his servant; it was a master, with the April wind's whims; and it had just played him a diabolical trick. The very jolt with which he came back to the schoolroom in the midst of his fancied flight jarred his day-dream utterly out of him; and he sat, open-mouthed in horror at what he had said.

The unanimous gasp of awe was protracted. Miss Spence, however, finally recovered her breath, and, returning deliberately to the platform, faced the school. "And then for a little while," as pathetic stories sometimes recount, "everything was very still." It was so still, in fact, that Penrod's new-born notoriety could almost be heard growing. This grisly silence was at last broken by the teacher.

"Penrod Schofield, stand up!"

The miserable child obeyed.

"What did you mean by speaking to me in that way?"

He hung his head, raked the floor with the side of his shoe, swayed, swallowed, looked suddenly at his hands with the air of never having seen them before, then clasped them behind him. The school shivered in ecstatic horror, every fascinated eye upon him; yet there was not a soul in the room but was profoundly grateful to him for the sensation—including the offended teacher herself. Unhappily, all this gratitude was unconscious and altogether different from the kind which, results in testimonials and loving-cups. On the contrary!

"Penrod Schofield!"

He gulped.

"Answer me at once! Why did you speak to me like that?"

"I was——" He choked, unable to continue.

"Speak out!"

"I was just—thinking," he managed to stammer.

"That will not do," she returned sharply. "I wish to know immediately why you spoke as you did."

The stricken Penrod answered helplessly:

"Because I was just thinking."

Upon the very rack he could have offered no ampler truthful explanation. It was all he knew about it.

"Thinking what?"

"Just thinking."

Miss Spence's expression gave evidence that her power of self-restraint was undergoing a remarkable test. However, after taking counsel with herself, she commanded:

"Come here!"

He shuffled forward, and she placed a chair upon the platform near her own.

"Sit there!"

Then (but not at all as if nothing had happened), she continued the lesson in arithmetic. Spiritually the children may have learned a lesson in very small fractions indeed as they gazed at the fragment of sin before them on the stool of penitence. They all stared at him attentively with hard and passionately interested eyes, in which there was never one trace of pity. It cannot be said with precision that he writhed; his movement was more a slow, continuous squirm, effected with a ghastly assumption of languid indifference; while his gaze, in the effort to escape the marble-hearted glare of his schoolmates, affixed itself with apparent permanence to the waistcoat button of James Russell Lowell just above the "U" in "Russell."

Classes came and classes went, grilling him with eyes. Newcomers received the story of the crime in darkling whispers; and the outcast sat and sat and sat, and squirmed and squirmed and squirmed. (He did one or two things with his spine which a professional contortionist would have observed with real interest.) And all this while of freezing suspense was but the criminal's detention awaiting trial. A known punishment may be anticipated with some measure of equanimity; at least, the prisoner may prepare himself to undergo it; but the unknown looms more monstrous for every attempt to guess it. Penrod's crime was unique; there were no rules to aid him in estimating the vengeance to fall upon him for it. What seemed most probable was that he would be expelled from the schools in the presence of his family, the mayor, and council, and afterward whipped by his father upon the State House steps, with the entire city as audience by invitation of the authorities.

Noon came. The rows of children filed out, every head turning for a last unpleasingly speculative look at the outlaw. Then Miss Spence closed the door into the cloakroom and that into the big hall, and came and sat at her desk, near Penrod. The tramping of feet outside, the shrill calls and shouting and the changing voices of the older boys ceased to be heard—and there was silence. Penrod, still affecting to be occupied with Lowell, was conscious that Miss Spence looked at him intently.

"Penrod," she said gravely, "what excuse have you to offer before I report your case to the principal?"

The word "principal" struck him to the vitals. Grand Inquisitor, Grand Khan, Sultan, Emperor, Tsar, Caesar Augustus—these are comparable. He stopped squirming instantly, and sat rigid.

"I want an answer. Why did you shout those words at me?"

"Well," he murmured, "I was just—thinking."

"Thinking what?" she asked sharply.

"I don't know."

"That won't do!"

He took his left ankle in his right hand and regarded it helplessly.

"That won't do, Penrod Schofield," she repeated severely. "If that is all the excuse you have to offer I shall report your case this instant!"

And she rose with fatal intent.

But Penrod was one of those whom the precipice inspires. "Well, I HAVE got an excuse."

"Well"—she paused impatiently—"what is it?"

He had not an idea, but he felt one coming, and replied automatically, in a plaintive tone:

"I guess anybody that had been through what I had to go through, last night, would think they had an excuse."

Miss Spence resumed her seat, though with the air of being ready to leap from it instantly.

"What has last night to do with your insolence to me this morning?"

"Well, I guess you'd see," he returned, emphasizing the plaintive note, "if you knew what I know."

"Now, Penrod," she said, in a kinder voice, "I have a high regard for your mother and father, and it would hurt me to distress them, but you must either tell me what was the matter with you or I'll have to take you to Mrs. Houston."

"Well, ain't I going to?" he cried, spurred by the dread name. "It's because I didn't sleep last night."

"Were you ill?" The question was put with some dryness.

He felt the dryness. "No'm; I wasn't."

"Then if someone in your family was so ill that even you were kept up all night, how does it happen they let you come to school this morning?"

"It wasn't illness," he returned, shaking his head mournfully. "It was lots worse'n anybody's being sick. It was—it was—well, it was jest awful."

"WHAT was?" He remarked with anxiety the incredulity in her tone.

"It was about Aunt Clara," he said.

"Your Aunt Clara!" she repeated. "Do you mean your mother's sister who married Mr. Farry of Dayton, Illinois?"

"Yes—Uncle John," returned Penrod sorrowfully. "The trouble was about him."

Miss Spence frowned a frown which he rightly interpreted as one of continued suspicion. "She and I were in school together," she said. "I used to know her very well, and I've always heard her married life was entirely happy. I don't——"

"Yes, it was," he interrupted, "until last year when Uncle John took to running with travelling men——"

"What?"

"Yes'm." He nodded solemnly. "That was what started it. At first he was a good, kind husband, but these travelling men would coax him into a saloon on his way home from work, and they got him to drinking beer and then ales, wines, liquors, and cigars——"

"Penrod!"

"Ma'am?"

"I'm not inquiring into your Aunt Clara's private affairs; I'm asking you if you have anything to say which would palliate——"

"That's what I'm tryin' to TELL you about, Miss Spence," he pleaded,—"if you'd jest only let me. When Aunt Clara and her little baby daughter got to our house last night——"

"You say Mrs. Farry is visiting your mother?"

"Yes'm—not just visiting—you see, she HAD to come. Well of course, little baby Clara, she was so bruised up and mauled, where he'd been hittin' her with his cane——"

"You mean that your uncle had done such a thing as THAT!" exclaimed Miss Spence, suddenly disarmed by this scandal.

"Yes'm, and mamma and Margaret had to sit up all night nursin' little Clara—and AUNT Clara was in such a state SOMEBODY had to keep talkin' to HER, and there wasn't anybody but me to do it, so I——"

"But where was your father?" she cried.

"Ma'am?"

"Where was your father while——"

"Oh—papa?" Penrod paused, reflected; then brightened. "Why, he was down at the train, waitin' to see if Uncle John would try to follow 'em and make 'em come home so's he could persecute 'em some more. I wanted to do that, but they said if he

did come I mightn't be strong enough to hold him and——" The brave lad paused again, modestly. Miss Spence's expression was encouraging. Her eyes were wide with astonishment, and there may have been in them, also, the mingled beginnings of admiration and self-reproach. Penrod, warming to his work, felt safer every moment.

"And so," he continued, "I had to sit up with Aunt Clara. She had some pretty big bruises, too, and I had to——"

"But why didn't they send for a doctor?" However, this question was only a flicker of dying incredulity.

"Oh, they didn't want any DOCTOR," exclaimed the inspired realist promptly. "They don't want anybody to HEAR about it because Uncle John might reform—and then where'd he be if everybody knew he'd been a drunkard and whipped his wife and baby daughter?"

"Oh!" said Miss Spence.

"You see, he used to be upright as anybody," he went on explanatively. "It all begun——"

"Began, Penrod."

"Yes'm. It all commenced from the first day he let those travelling men coax him into the saloon." Penrod narrated the downfall of his Uncle John at length. In detail he was nothing short of plethoric; and incident followed incident, sketched with such vividness, such abundance of colour, and such verisimilitude to a drunkard's life as a drunkard's life should be, that had Miss Spence possessed the rather chilling attributes of William J. Burns himself, the last trace of skepticism must have vanished from her mind.

Besides, there are two things that will be believed of any man whatsoever, and one of them is that he has taken to drink. And in every sense it was a moving picture which, with simple but eloquent words, the virtuous Penrod set before his teacher.

His eloquence increased with what it fed on; and as with the eloquence so with self-reproach in the gentle bosom of the teacher. She cleared her throat with difficulty once or twice, during his description of his ministering night with Aunt Clara. "And I said to her, 'Why, Aunt Clara, what's the use of takin' on so about it?' And I said, 'Now, Aunt Clara, all the crying in the world can't make things any better.' And then she'd just keep catchin' hold of me, and sob and kind of holler, and I'd say, 'DON'T cry, Aunt Clara—PLEASE don't cry.'"

Then, under the influence of some fragmentary survivals of the respectable portion of his Sunday adventures, his theme became more exalted; and, only partially misquoting a phrase from a psalm, he related how he had made it of comfort to Aunt Clara, and how he had besought her to seek Higher guidance in her trouble.

The surprising thing about a structure such as Penrod was erecting is that the taller it becomes the more ornamentation it will stand. Gifted boys have this faculty of building magnificence upon cobwebs—and Penrod was gifted. Under the spell of his really great performance, Miss Spence gazed more and more sweetly upon the prodigy of spiritual beauty and goodness before her, until at last, when Penrod came to the explanation of his "just thinking," she was forced to turn her head away.

"You mean, dear," she said gently, "that you were all worn out and hardly knew what you were saying?"

"Yes'm."

"And you were thinking about all those dreadful things so hard that you forgot where you were?"

"I was thinking," he said simply, "how to save Uncle John."

And the end of it for this mighty boy was that the teacher kissed him!

CHAPTER XI
FIDELITY OF A LITTLE DOG

THE RETURNING STUDENTS, THAT afternoon, observed that Penrod's desk was vacant—and nothing could have been more impressive than that sinister mere emptiness. The accepted theory was that Penrod had been arrested. How breathtaking, then, the sensation when, at the beginning of the second hour, he strolled—in with inimitable carelessness and, rubbing his eyes, somewhat noticeably in the manner of one who has snatched an hour of much needed sleep, took his place as if nothing in particular had happened. This, at first supposed to be a superhuman exhibition of sheer audacity, became but the more dumfounding when Miss Spence—looking up from her desk—greeted him with a pleasant little nod. Even after school, Penrod gave numerous maddened investigators no relief. All he would consent to say was:

"Oh, I just TALKED to her."

A mystification not entirely unconnected with the one thus produced was manifested at his own family dinner-table the following evening. Aunt Clara had been out rather late, and came to the table after the rest were seated. She wore a puzzled expression.

"Do you ever see Mary Spence nowadays?" she inquired, as she unfolded her napkin, addressing Mrs. Schofield. Penrod abruptly set down his soup-spoon and gazed at his aunt with flattering attention.

"Yes; sometimes," said Mrs. Schofield. "She's Penrod's teacher."

"Is she?" said Mrs. Farry. "Do you—" She paused. "Do people think her a little—queer, these days?"

"Why, no," returned her sister. "What makes you say that?"

"She has acquired a very odd manner," said Mrs. Farry decidedly. "At least, she seemed odd to ME. I met her at the corner just before I got to the house, a few minutes ago, and after we'd said howdy-do to each other, she kept hold of my hand and looked as though she was going to cry. She seemed to be trying to say something, and choking——"

"But I don't think that's so very queer, Clara. She knew you in school, didn't she?"

"Yes, but——"

"And she hadn't seen you for so many years, I think it's perfectly natural she——"

"Wait! She stood there squeezing my hand, and struggling to get her voice—and I got really embarrassed—and then finally she said, in a kind of tearful whisper, 'Be of good cheer—this trial will pass!'"

"How queer!" exclaimed Margaret.

Penrod sighed, and returned somewhat absently to his soup.

"Well, I don't know," said Mrs. Schofield thoughtfully. "Of course she's heard about the outbreak of measles in Dayton, since they had to close the schools, and she knows you live there——"

"But doesn't it seem a VERY exaggerated way," suggested Margaret, "to talk about measles?"

"Wait!" begged Aunt Clara. "After she said that, she said something even queerer, and then put her handkerchief to her eyes and hurried away."

Penrod laid down his spoon again and moved his chair slightly back from the table. A spirit of prophecy was upon him: he knew that someone was going to ask a question which he felt might better remain unspoken.

"What WAS the other thing she said?" Mr. Schofield inquired, thus immediately fulfilling his son's premonition.

"She said," returned Mrs. Farry slowly, looking about the table, "she said, 'I know that Penrod is a great, great comfort to you!'"

There was a general exclamation of surprise. It was a singular thing, and in no manner may it be considered complimentary to Penrod, that this speech of Miss Spence's should have immediately confirmed Mrs. Farry's doubts about her in the minds of all his family.

Mr. Schofield shook his head pityingly.

"I'm afraid she's a goner," he went so far as to say.

"Of all the weird ideas!" cried Margaret.

"I never heard anything like it in my life!" Mrs. Schofield exclaimed. "Was that ALL she said?"

"Every word!"

Penrod again resumed attention to his soup. His mother looked at him curiously, and then, struck by a sudden thought, gathered the glances of the adults of the table by a significant movement of the head, and, by another, conveyed an admonition to drop the subject until later. Miss Spence was Penrod's teacher: it was better, for many reasons, not to discuss the subject of her queerness before him. This was Mrs. Schofield's thought at the time. Later she had another, and it kept her awake.

The next afternoon, Mr. Schofield, returning at five o'clock from the cares of the day, found the house deserted, and sat down to read his evening paper in what appeared to be an uninhabited apartment known to its own world as the "drawing-room." A sneeze, unexpected both to him and the owner, informed him of the presence of another person.

"Where are you, Penrod?" the parent asked, looking about.

"Here," said Penrod meekly.

Stooping, Mr. Schofield discovered his son squatting under the piano, near an open window—his wistful Duke lying beside him.

"What are you doing there?"

"Me?"

"Why under the piano?"

"Well," the boy returned, with grave sweetness, "I was just kind of sitting here—thinking."

"All right." Mr. Schofield, rather touched, returned to the digestion of a murder, his back once more to the piano; and Penrod silently drew from beneath his jacket (where he had slipped it simultaneously with the sneeze) a paper-backed volume entitled: "Slimsy, the Sioux City Squealer, or, 'Not Guilty, Your Honor.'"

In this manner the reading-club continued in peace, absorbed, contented, the world well forgot—until a sudden, violently irritated slam-bang of the front door startled the members; and Mrs. Schofield burst into the room and threw herself into a chair, moaning.

"What's the matter, mamma?" asked her husband laying aside his paper.

"Henry Passloe Schofield," returned the lady, "I don't know what IS to be done with that boy; I do NOT!"

"You mean Penrod?"

"Who else could I mean?" She sat up, exasperated, to stare at him. "Henry Passloe Schofield, you've got to take this matter in your hands—it's beyond me!"

"Well, what has he——"

"Last night I got to thinking," she began rapidly, "about what Clara told us—thank Heaven she and Margaret and little Clara have gone to tea at Cousin Charlotte's!—but they'll be home soon—about what she said about Miss Spence——"

"You mean about Penrod's being a comfort?"

"Yes, and I kept thinking and thinking and thinking about it till I couldn't stand it any——"

"By GEORGE!" shouted Mr. Schofield startlingly, stooping to look under the piano. A statement that he had suddenly remembered his son's presence would be lacking in accuracy, for the highly sensitized Penrod was, in fact, no longer present. No more was Duke, his faithful dog.

"What's the matter?"

"Nothing," he returned, striding to the open window and looking out. "Go on."

"Oh," she moaned, "it must be kept from Clara—and I'll never hold up my head again if John Farry ever hears of it!"

"Hears of WHAT?"

"Well, I just couldn't stand it, I got so curious; and I thought of course if Miss Spence HAD become a little unbalanced it was my duty to know it, as Penrod's mother and she his teacher; so I thought I would just call on her at her apartment after school and have a chat and see and I did and—oh——"

"Well?"

"I've just come from there, and she told me—she told me! Oh, I've NEVER known anything like this!"

"WHAT did she tell you?"

Mrs. Schofield, making a great effort, managed to assume a temporary appearance of calm. "Henry," she said solemnly, "bear this in mind: whatever you do to Penrod, it must be done in some place when Clara won't hear it. But the first thing to do is to find him."

Within view of the window from which Mr. Schofield was gazing was the closed door of the storeroom in the stable, and just outside this door Duke was performing a most engaging trick.

His young master had taught Duke to "sit up and beg" when he wanted anything, and if that didn't get it, to "speak." Duke was facing the closed door and sitting up and begging, and now he also spoke—in a loud, clear bark.

There was an open transom over the door, and from this descended—hurled by an unseen agency—a can half filled with old paint.

It caught the small besieger of the door on his thoroughly surprised right ear, encouraged him to some remarkable acrobatics, and turned large portions of him a dull blue. Allowing only a moment to perplexity, and deciding, after a single and evidently unappetizing experiment, not to cleanse himself of paint, the loyal animal resumed his quaint, upright posture.

Mr. Schofield seated himself on the window-sill, whence he could keep in view that pathetic picture of unrequited love.

"Go on with your story, mamma," he said. "I think I can find Penrod when we want him."

And a few minutes later he added, "And I think I know the place to do it in."

Again the faithful voice of Duke was heard, pleading outside the bolted door.

TO BE CONTINUED IN LITERARY OUTLAW #4

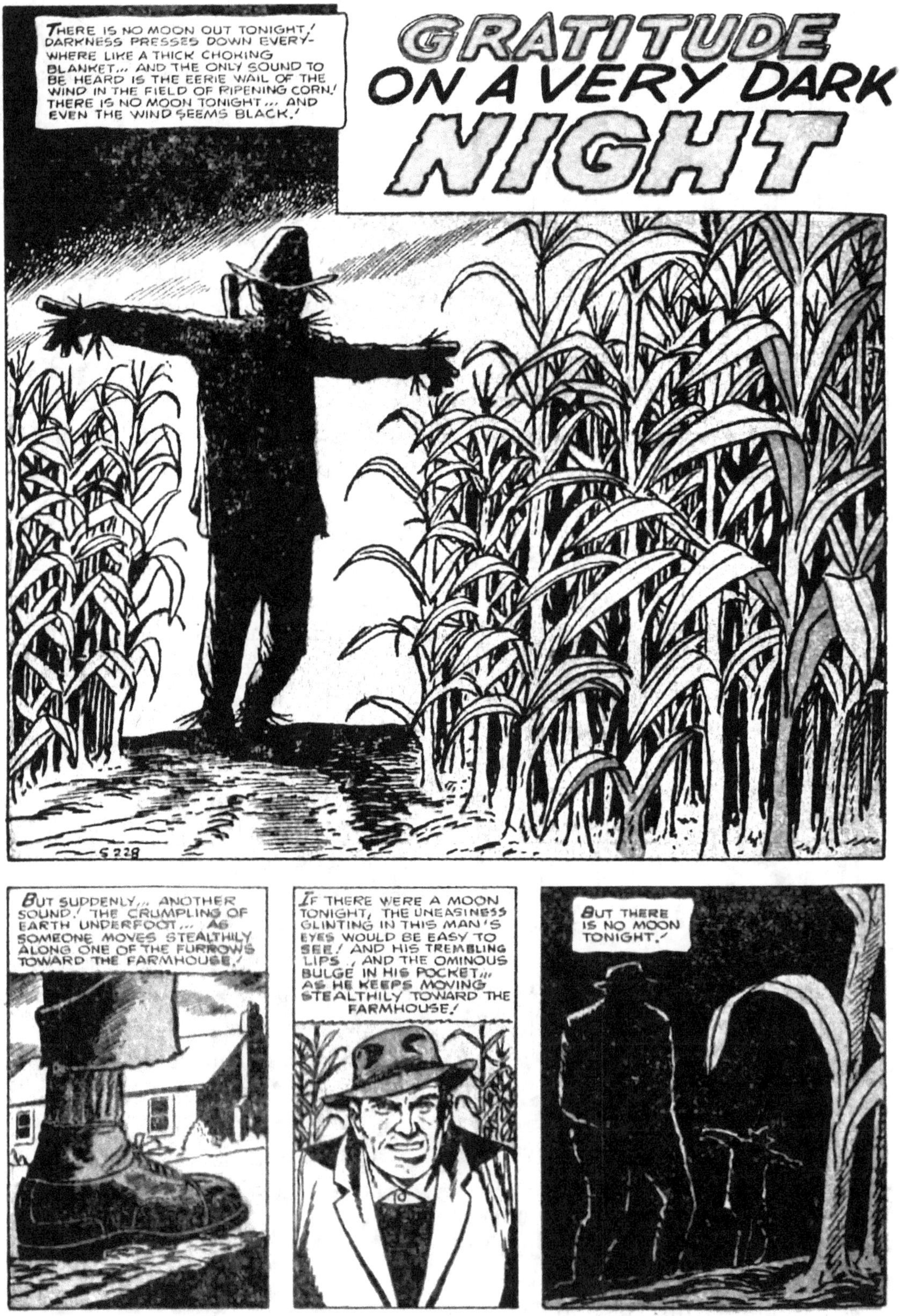

GRATITUDE ON A VERY DARK NIGHT

INSIDE THE FARMHOUSE, SLEEPING PEACEFULLY, IS OLD JOHN DUNN, A MAN WHO HAS NEVER HARMED A SOUL! WHO HAS ALWAYS TREATED EVERY LIVING BEING, INCLUDING FAMILY, FRIENDS, NEIGHBORS, EVEN STRANGERS, EVEN THE LIVE-STOCK ON HIS FARM, EVEN THE SCARECROW...

... WITH THE SAME GENTLE KINDNESS.'
HOW COME YOU'RE CHANGING IT, JOHN? HE CAN'T FEEL THE COLD.'
GUESS HE CAN'T AT THAT...!

... BUT JUST THE THOUGHT OF HIM STANDING OUT HERE NIGHT AFTER NIGHT WITH THE COLD WIND WHISTLING THROUGH ALL THE HOLES IN THIS OLD COAT, IS ENOUGH TO GIVE ME THE SHIVERS!

IT'S NOT THAT I'M SO TOUCHED IN THE HEAD, SHERIFF, AS TO THINK HIM ALIVE.' BUT AFTER ALL, HE'S MADE IN THE SHAPE OF A MAN ... AND I AM GRATEFUL TO HIM FOR WATCHING MY CORN AS WELL AS HE DOES ... SO WHY NOT GIVE HIM A WARM COAT ON THE SLIM CHANCE THAT IT MIGHT MAKE SOME DIFFERENCE?

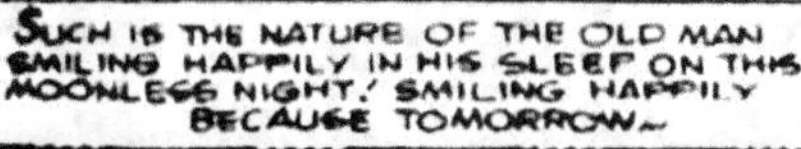

SUCH IS THE NATURE OF THE OLD MAN SMILING HAPPILY IN HIS SLEEP ON THIS MOONLESS NIGHT.' SMILING HAPPILY BECAUSE TOMORROW~

... HE WILL ATTEND THE WEDDING OF HIS ONLY GRAND-CHILD.' AND HE WILL GIVE HER A PRESENT THAT WILL BE MORE THAN ENOUGH TO GIVE HER AND HER YOUNG HUSBAND A GOOD START IN LIFE.' A PRESENT COMPRISED OF ALL THE MONEY OLD JOHN HAS EVER MANAGED TO PUT ASIDE ... HIS ENTIRE SAVINGS, WITHDRAWN BY HIM FROM THE BANK JUST THAT AFTERNOON.'

THAT IS THE MONEY, TIED IN A NEAT BUNDLE, ON THE BUREAU BESIDE OLD JOHN'S BED... ON THIS MOONLESS NIGHT!

MEANWHILE, OUT IN THE FIELD OF DARK RIPENING CORN...
I HATE TO DO THIS! ALMOST WISH I HADN'T SPOTTED THE OLD MAN MAKING THE BIG WITHDRAWAL AT THE BANK TODAY!

IF IT ONLY COULD'VE BEEN SOMEBODY ELSE! HE'S SUCH A DECENT OLD GUY! BUT I NEED MONEY!

HEY?! WHO'S THAT....?!

WHEW! FOR A SECOND I THOUGHT.... BUT IT'S ONLY A SCARECROW!

HAVE TO PULL MYSELF TOGETHER! I NEED THAT DOUGH.. HAVE TO STOP THINKING HOW DECENT OLD MAN DUNN IS!

THAT WAD OF DOUGH IS AS GOOD AS IN MY POCKET RIGHT NOW.!

BUT SUDDENLY....
GASP.!

THE SCARECROW'S SHADOW... WITH ONE ARM UP... LIKE IT WAS TELLING ME TO STOP.!

I-I MUST BE SEEING THINGS... THAT SCARECROW'S ARMS ARE STRAIGHT OUT... BOTH OF THEM.!
BUT THE SHADOW STILL HAS ONE ARM UP.!

I'LL GO THE LONG WAY... DOWN ONE OF THE SIDE FURROWS.! THAT WAY I WON'T SEE...

TH-THIS JUST CAN'T BE.! IT JUST CAN'T BE FOLLOWING ME.!

STOP.! STOP FOLLOWING ME.!
BLAM!
BLAM!
BLAM!
BLAM!

STOP! OH, PLEASE (SOB) STOP FOLLOWING ME! HELP!

... HELP! HELP!
THAT YELLING'S COMING FROM OLD JOHN DUNN'S CORNFIELD! LET'S GO SEE WHAT IT'S ALL ABOUT!

IN THE MORNING...
...THAT'S RIGHT, JOHN! HE WAS CAUGHT IN YOUR FIELD LAST NIGHT! HE WAS SO SCARED THAT HE CONFESSED HE MEANT TO ROB YOU! ... SCARED BY WHAT?...
...BY YOUR SCARECROW'S SHADOW, HE CLAIMS...!

WHAT'S THAT, JOHN?...
HEY! I HADN'T THOUGHT OF THAT! BUT IT'S SO....
THERE WAS NO MOON LAST NIGHT! THE SCARECROW COULDN'T POSSIBLY HAVE CAST A SHADOW!

NO MOON LAST NIGHT... AND JUST ONE SCARECROW BETWEEN THAT CROOK AND OLD JOHN DUNN! ONE SCARECROW THAT OLD JOHN HAD SHOWN HIS GRATITUDE TO! COULD IT BE THAT IT FELT GRATITUDE TOO? THAT THROWING THE SCARY SHADOW WAS THE ONLY WAY IT COULD SHOW ITS GRATITUDE?

COULD IT BE? OR COULD IT HAVE BEEN THE CROOK'S CONSCIENCE?... GUESS WE'LL NEVER KNOW...!

THE WHITE SHIP
BY H. P. LOVECRAFT

I AM BASIL ELTON, KEEPER OF THE North Point light that my father and grandfather kept before me. Far from the shore stands the grey lighthouse, above sunken slimy rocks that are seen when the tide is low, but unseen when the tide is high. Past that beacon for a century have swept the majestic barques of the seven seas. In the days of my grandfather there were many; in the days of my father not so many; and now there are so few that I sometimes feel strangely alone, as though I were the last man on our planet.

From far shores came those white-sailed argosies of old; from far Eastern shores where warm suns shine and sweet odours linger about strange gardens and gay temples. The old captains of the sea came often to my grandfather and told him of these things, which in turn he told to my father, and my father told to me in the long autumn evenings when the wind howled eerily from the East. And I have read more of these things, and of many things besides, in the books men gave me when I was young and filled with wonder.

But more wonderful than the lore of old men and the lore of books is the secret lore of ocean. Blue, green, grey, white or black; smooth, ruffled, or mountainous; that ocean is not silent.

All my days have I watched it and listened to it, and I know it well. At first it told to me only the plain little tales of calm beaches and near ports, but with the years it grew more friendly and spoke of other things; of things more strange and more distant in space and in time. Sometimes at twilight the grey vapours of the horizon have parted to grant me glimpses of the ways beyond; and sometimes at night the deep waters of the sea have grown clear and phosphorescent, to grant me glimpses of the ways beneath. And these glimpses have been as often of the ways that were and the ways that might be, as of the ways that are; for ocean is more ancient than the mountains, and freighted with the memories and the dreams of Time.

Out of the South it was that the White Ship used to come when the moon was full and high in the heavens. Out of the South it would glide very smoothly and silently over the sea. And whether the sea was rough or calm, and whether the wind was friendly or adverse, it would always glide smoothly and silently, its sails distent and its long strange tiers of oars moving rhythmically. One night I espied upon the deck a man, bearded and robed, and he seemed to beckon me to embark for fair unknown shores. Many times afterward I saw him under the full moon, and ever did he beckon me.

Very brightly did the moon shine on the night I answered the call, and I walked out over the waters to the White Ship on a bridge of moonbeams. The man who had beckoned now spoke a welcome to me in a soft language I seemed to know well, and the hours were filled with soft songs of the oarsmen as we glided away into a mysterious South, golden with the glow of that full, mellow moon.

And when the day dawned, rosy and effulgent, I beheld the green shore of far lands, bright and beautiful, and to me unknown. Up from the sea rose lordly terraces of verdure, tree-studded, and showing here and there the gleaming white roofs and colonnades of strange temples. As we drew nearer the green shore the bearded man told me of that land, the Land of Zar, where dwell all the dreams and thoughts of beauty that come to men once and then are forgotten. And when I looked upon the terraces again I saw that what he said was true, for among the sights before me were many things I had once seen through the mists beyond the horizon in the phosphorescent depths of ocean. There too were forms and fantasies more splendid than I had ever known; the visions of young poets who died in want before the world could learn of what they had seen and dreamed. But we did not set foot upon the sloping meadows of Zar, for it is told that he who treads them may nevermore return to his native shore.

As the White Ship sailed silently away from the templed terraces of Zar, we beheld on the distant horizon ahead the spires of a mighty city; and the bearded man said to me, "This is Thalarion, the City of a Thousand Wonders, wherein reside all those mysteries that man has striven in vain to fathom." And I looked again, at closer range, and saw that the city was greater than any city I had known or dreamed of before. Into the sky the spires of its temples reached, so that no man might behold their peaks; and far back beyond the horizon stretched the grim, grey walls, over which one might spy only a few roofs, weird and ominous, yet adorned with rich friezes and alluring sculptures. I yearned mightily to enter this fascinating yet repellent city, and beseeched the bearded man to land me at the stone pier by the huge carven gate Akariel; but he gently denied my wish, saying, "Into Thalarion, the City of a Thousand Wonders, many have passed but none returned. Therein walk only dæmons and mad things that are no longer men, and the streets are white with the unburied bones of those who have looked upon the eidolon Lathi, that reigns over the city." So the White Ship sailed on past the walls of Thalarion, and followed for many days a southward-flying bird, whose glossy plumage matched the sky out of which it had appeared.

Then came we to a pleasant coast gay with blossoms of every hue, where as far inland as we could see basked lovely groves and radiant arbours beneath a meridian sun. From bowers beyond our view came bursts of song and snatches of lyric harmony, interspersed with faint laughter so delicious that I urged the rowers onward in my eagerness to reach the scene. And the bearded man spoke no word, but watched me as we approached the lily-lined shore. Suddenly a wind blowing from over the flowery meadows and leafy woods brought a scent at which I trembled. The wind grew stronger, and the air was filled with the lethal, charnel odour of plague-stricken towns and uncovered cemeteries. And as we sailed madly away from that damnable coast the bearded man spoke at last, saying, "This is Xura, the Land of Pleasures Unattained."

So once more the White Ship followed the bird of heaven, over warm blessed seas fanned by caressing, aromatic breezes. Day after day and night after night did we sail, and when the moon was full we would listen to soft songs of the oarsmen, sweet as on that distant night when we sailed away from my far native land. And it was by moonlight that we anchored at last in the harbour of Sona-Nyl, which is guarded by twin headlands of crystal that rise from the sea and meet in a resplendent arch. This is the Land of Fancy, and we walked to the verdant shore upon a golden bridge of moonbeams.

In the Land of Sona-Nyl there is neither time nor space, neither suffering nor death; and there I dwelt for many æons. Green are the groves and pastures, bright and fragrant the flowers, blue and musical the streams, clear and cool the fountains, and stately and gorgeous the temples, castles, and cities of Sona-Nyl. Of that land there is no bound, for beyond each vista of beauty rises another more beautiful. Over the countryside and amidst the splendour of cities can move at will the happy folk, of whom all are gifted with unmarred grace and unalloyed happiness. For the æons that I dwelt there I wandered blissfully through gardens where quaint pagodas peep from pleasing clumps of bushes, and where the white walks are bordered with delicate blossoms. I climbed gentle hills from whose summits I could see entrancing panoramas of loveliness, with steepled towns nestling in verdant valleys, and with the golden domes of gigantic cities glittering on the infinitely distant horizon. And I viewed by moonlight the sparkling sea, the crystal headlands, and the placid harbour wherein lay anchored the White Ship.

It was against the full moon one night in the immemorial year of Tharp that I saw outlined the beckoning form of the celestial bird, and felt the first stirrings of unrest. Then I spoke with the bearded man, and told him of my new yearning to depart for remote Cathuria, which no man hath seen, but which all believe to lie beyond the basalt pillars of the West. It is the Land of Hope, and in it shine the perfect ideals of all that we know elsewhere; or at least so men relate. But the bearded man said to me, "Beware of those perilous seas wherein men say Cathuria lies. In Sona-Nyl there is no pain nor death, but who can tell what lies beyond the basalt pillars of the West?" Natheless at the next full moon I boarded the White Ship, and with the reluctant bearded man left the happy harbour for untravelled seas.

And the bird of heaven flew before, and led us toward the basalt pillars of the West, but this time the oarsmen sang no soft songs under the full moon. In my mind I would often picture the unknown Land of Cathuria with its splendid groves and palaces, and would wonder what new delights there awaited me. "Cathuria," I would say to myself, "is the abode of gods and the land of unnumbered cities of gold. Its forests are of aloe and sandalwood, even as the fragrant groves of Camorin, and among the trees flutter gay birds sweet with song. On the green and flowery mountains of Cathuria stand temples of pink marble, rich with carven and painted glories, and having in their courtyards cool fountains of silver, where purl with ravishing music the scented waters that come from the grotto-born river Narg. And the cities of Cathuria are cinctured with golden walls, and their pavements are also of gold. In the gardens of these cities are strange orchids, and perfumed lakes whose beds are of coral and amber. At night the streets and the gardens are lit with gay lanterns fashioned from three-coloured shell of the tortoise, and here resound the soft notes of the singer and the lutanist. And the houses of the cities of Cathuria are all palaces, each built over a fragrant canal bearing the waters of the sacred Narg. Of marble and porphyry are the houses, and roofed with glittering gold that reflects the rays of the sun and enhances the splendour of the cities as blissful gods view them from the distant peaks.

Fairest of all is the palace of the great monarch Dorieb, whom some say to be a demigod and others a god. High is the palace of Dorieb, and many are the turrets of marble upon its walls. In its wide halls may multitudes assemble, and here hang the trophies of the ages. And the roof is of pure gold, set upon tall pillars of ruby and azure, and having such carven figures of gods and heroes that he who looks up to those heights seem to gaze upon the living Olympus. And the floor of the palace is of glass, under which flow the cunningly lighted waters of the Narg, gay with gaudy fish not known beyond the bounds of lovely Cathuria."

Thus would I speak to myself of Cathuria, but ever would the bearded man warn me to turn back to the happy shores of Sona-Nyl; for Sona-Nyl is known of men, while none hath ever beheld Cathuria.

And on the thirty-first day that we followed the bird, we beheld the basalt pillars of the West. Shrouded in mist they were, so that no man might peer beyond them or see their summits—which indeed some say reach even to the heavens. And the bearded man again implored me to turn back, but I heeded him not; for from the mists beyond the basalt pillars I fancied there came the notes of singer and lutanist; sweeter than the sweetest songs of Sona-Nyl, and sounding mine own praises; the praises of me, who had voyaged far under the full moon and dwelt in the Land of Fancy.

So to the sound of melody the White Ship sailed into the mist betwixt the basalt pillars of the West.

And when the music ceased and the mist lifted, we beheld not the Land of Cathuria, but a swift-rushing resistless sea, over which our helpless barque was borne toward some unknown goal. Soon to our ears came the distant thunder of falling waters, and to our eyes appeared on the far horizon ahead the titanic spray of a monstrous cataract, wherein the oceans of the world drop down to abysmal nothingness. Then did the bearded man say to me with tears on his cheek, "We have rejected the beautiful Land of Sona-Nyl, which we may never behold again. The gods are greater than men, and they have conquered." And I closed my eyes before the crash that I knew would come, shutting out the sight of the celestial bird which flapped its mocking blue wings over the brink of the torrent.

Out of that crash came darkness, and I heard the shrieking of men and of things which were not men. From the East tempestuous winds arose, and chilled me as I crouched on the slab of damp stone which had risen beneath my feet. Then as I heard another crash I opened my eyes and beheld myself upon the platform of that lighthouse from whence I had sailed so many æons ago. In the darkness below there loomed the vast blurred outlines of a vessel breaking up on the cruel rocks, and as I glanced out over the waste I saw that the light had failed for the first time since my grandfather had assumed its care.

And in the later watches of the night, when I went within the tower, I saw on the wall a calendar which still remained as when I had left it at the hour I sailed away. With the dawn I descended the tower and looked for wreckage upon the rocks, but what I found was only this: a strange dead bird whose hue was as of the azure sky, and a single shattered spar, of a whiteness greater than that of the wave-tips or of the mountain snow.

And thereafter the ocean told me its secrets no more; and though many times since has the moon shone full and high in the heavens, the White Ship from the South came never again.

THE END

"THE OLDEST AND STRONGEST EMOTION OF MANKIND IS FEAR, AND THE OLDEST AND STRONGEST KIND OF FEAR IS FEAR OF THE UNKNOWN."
— H. P. LOVECRAFT

THE ANVIL OF JOVE

An exterior monologue for voice and two cymbals

I am the Anvil of Jove.
I smash evil,
I am the Anvil of Jove,
I opened the door,
I smash evil,
just a little, I opened the door,
And your mother was in bed,
your mother was in bed,
she was in bed,
she was just in bed,
I opened the door very slowly,
very slowly it creaked open,
and your mother was in bed,
I am your mother's lover
and you have no father,
but your mother was in bed with her lover,
she was in bed with her lover,
And I am her lover,
I saw her there in bed with her lover,
I am the Anvil of Jove,
I smash evil,
and your mother was in bed
with her lover,
with her lover,
and I am your mother's lover,
but she was in bed,
and the light hit her,
and she was in bed,
I smash evil,
and I saw her in bed,
and I went to the bed,
And I killed her and her lover,
I smashed her head and her lover's head,
I hit her with a hammer,
your mother is dead,

your mother's lover is dead,
and I am your mother's lover,
your mother was dead,
your mother was dead,
and the sheets were all covered with her blood,
and your mother's lover was dead,
And I smash evil,
Your mother's lover was dead,
I am the Anvil of Jove,
I am your mother's lover,
I smash evil,
The blood stained the sheets and the floor,
I smashed her lover's head,
I saw in the mirror
as my hand went up and down,
I killed your mother,
and I killed your mother's lover,
I am the Anvil of Jove,
I opened the door,
and I saw her there,
very slowly I opened the door,
I saw her there lying in her sheeted blood,
and her lover all bloody,
I am your mother's lover
and your mother
and your mother
and your mother's lover is dead,
I am the Anvil of Jove
who is your mother's lover
I am your mother's lover
who is dead,
who is lying in his own blood,
who is lying in her blood,
who are lying in their blood,
I am your mother's lover
who is . . .
who is . . .
who is dead.
Who is dead?
I am dead?
I am dead!
I am your mother's lover,
and you mother's lover is dead,

dead in his own blood and her own blood,
dead,
and I am he,
so I must be dead,
I am dead,
I am your mother's lover,
your mother's lover   I am dead
I am dead,
I am dead,
I am dead,
because I am your mother's lover
I am dead,
I am the Anvil of Jove
I smash evil,
Your mother was evil,
your mother's lover who is me is evil,
was evil,
I smashed your mother and her lover,
and they are dead in their blood,
I am dead,
and I am telling you that I am.

And he dropped the hammer and clutched his bloodied head
ran down the steps,
into the bushes,
and slept away into the night
and into the day . . .

— Steven Riddle
October 1978

CONTRIBUTORS

JOHN GRAVES publishes Literary Outlaw magazine and hosts the Literary Outlaw podcast. He lives on a working farm in the shadow of the Blue Ridge Mountains in Virginia. He's half southern, half yankee, and all American. He describes himself as an Ecclesiastes 1:17 man married to a Proverbs 31 woman. John is the author of the *Starship Gilead* trilogy and the forthcoming weird western series *Rook: God's Gunslinger.*

BRUCE JONES is an American comic book writer, novelist, illustrator, and screenwriter whose work included writing Marvel Comics' *The Incredible Hulk* and DC Comics' *Nightwing.*

H. P. LOVECRAFT (1890 – 1937) was an American writer of weird, science, fantasy, and horror fiction. He is best known for his creation of the Cthulhu Mythos.

STEVEN RIDDLE is a poet living in central Florida where constant communion with ibises, Sand Hill cranes, herons, egrets, and anhingas has allowed him to rack up literally thousands of poems. Would you like some?

EDWIN ARLINGTON ROBINSON (1869 – 1935) was an American poet and playwright. Robinson won the Pulitzer Prize for Poetry on three occasions and was nominated for the Nobel Prize in Literature four times.

PERCY BYSSHE SHELLEY (1792 – 1822) was a British writer who is considered as one of the major English Romantic poets.

BOOTH TARKINGTON (1869 – 1946) was an American novelist and dramatist best known for his novels The Magnificent Ambersons (1918) and Alice Adams (1921). He is one of only four novelists to win the Pulitzer Prize for Fiction more than once.

KAREN TRAVISS is a science fiction author from Wiltshire, England. She is the author of the *Wess'Har* and *Nomad* series, and has written tie-in material based on *Star Wars, Gears of War, Halo, and G.I. Joe.*

THORNTON WILDER (1897 – 1975) was an American playwright and novelist. He won three Pulitzer Prizes for the novel *The Bridge of San Luis Rey* and for the plays *Our Town* and *The Skin of Our Teeth.*

MARV WOLFMAN is an American comic book and novelization writer. He worked on Marvel Comics's *The Tomb of Dracula,* for which he and artist Gene Colan created the vampire-slayer *Blade*, and DC Comics's *The New Teen Titans* and the *Crisis on Infinite Earths* limited series with George Pérez.